I don't *always* end up half-naked in a cab in the Bronx when I go out. It's just that, well, I sometimes do. And twice is apparently two times too many, if my father is to be believed.

"Ada, this has to stop."

"I know."

There was no point in making excuses. We had been through too much for that, both of us.

Dad sat down opposite me on my blue velvet couch. His wedding band slid along his ring finger. He still hadn't gained back the weight he lost after Max.

"Ada. What do you want me to do? What can I do?"

I forced a smile for his benefit. There was so much, and all of it too little and far too late. "I'm fine, Dad. Truly. Don't worry about me."

He stood abruptly and moved to the windows. The bare branches of Central Park were heavy with snow.

"I can't lose you too." He spoke to the city, as if it were easier to face than me. "I just can't. Ada, you're turning twenty-four next year. It's been a year since your graduation and nearly two years since Max."

"Two and a half." Two years, seven months and four days, to be exact.

"I don't care much for how you spend your days, but it's your nights that worry me. I won't lose you as well."

"You won't," I said, playing with a thread in my sleeve. Somehow I needed him to realize that the partying, surrounding myself with people—it was a survival mechanism. It wasn't personal.

"I want you to accompany me to the Hathaway's New Year's ball tonight."

"No, Dad, I can't—"

"And starting Monday next week, I will make sure you can start an internship at Hathaway's."

"No, thank you. I'm not interested," I ground out. He had the best intentions, of that I had no doubt, despite not knowing how to communicate with me. He'd never been too good at doing that with his children.

"It's not an offer. It's an ultimatum. Addie, I'm making the access to your trust fund dependent on this."

"On this internship?"

"You were to gain access at age twenty-five, but I'm adding a three-month internship at Hathaway's first as an addendum. I've already been in contact with the lawyers. I want you dressed and ready at nine tonight for the event, and then at work at eight o'clock every morning."

I gave a vain tug at my silk bathrobe. He'd showed up, unannounced, and it was only two in the afternoon. So what if I was still in my PJs? Cheap shot.

"What division?"

I knew better than to get vocal and angry with Dad. It'd never been the way to win an argument with him. Max had known how to make our case, methodically and empirically, but he was gone.

"Executive," Dad said. "I'm going to ask Grant to supervise your internship."

I flew up from my seat. "What? *Grant*? There is absolutely *no* way I will work in close contact with him."

Dad sighed. He looked disappointed, but then again, I

Edited by Stephanie Parent
www.oliviahayle.com

OLIVIA HAYLE

found it hard to remember him ever wearing any other expression.

"He is the CEO and executive partner of the auction house. I trust him. There is absolutely no one else I would entrust to oversee your internship."

I gave him a small pout and my very best, saddest eyes. "Please, not him."

Grant. The man had never smiled in his life. I couldn't handle him being my overseer.

We would tear each other apart.

"You're only proving my point, Ada. I can't give you and your antics to just anyone. They'd either kill you or worship at your feet within a week."

"And you think Grant won't?"

Dad opened his briefcase, taking out a stack of documents and placing them on my granite countertop. "I know he won't, try as you may."

Dad's trust in Grant was like an owner's belief in their well-mannered dog. *Don't worry, he won't bite.*

I gave a sudden smile. Maybe I could push Grant far enough for him to snap.

"I want you to read through this before Monday," Dad said. "It's an overview of all of the firm's divisions and background info of the main real estate, art and artifacts that have been sold in the past year. I suggest you read up on it."

I knew he was waiting for me to say thank you, but for the life of me, I couldn't force myself to speak the words. There was so much I had wanted from him, for so long, but the past few years had made it painfully clear that I'd never get it. So I remained quiet.

Dad coughed and rubbed the back of his neck. "Well then, I suppose I'll be off. I'll see you tonight—I'll be outside in the car at nine. And Ada?"

"Yes?"

"Don't screw this up. You won't get any more chances like this."

The door shut behind him, and my apartment was once again quiet, empty and lonely. I sighed and grabbed the stack of documents—and a bowl of cereal—before nestling down on the couch.

Working with Grant. The man hated me, had never been able to stand that his perfect mentor had somehow produced two less than perfect children. Obsessed with his achievements and numbers.

I smiled, thinking about the many times we'd sparred in the past. It had been a long time since we'd had one of our verbal duels.

These months were likely going to be excruciating, nerve-racking, angering and a hundred percent sure to go wrong.

It might just be the most fun I'd had in years.

2

___

GRANT

It was four thirty and I'd finished outlining the coming week with Linda when my former mentor knocked on the door. The next board meeting wasn't for another week. What was he doing in the city?

"Arthur?"

"Grant." He gave me a wide smile. He'd always been kinder to me than I deserved. "I'm sorry to bother you unannounced like this. I know your days are busy."

He sat down in the sleek chair opposite my desk, crossing his legs.

"I always have time for you."

The old man had been an inspiration to me for years—longer than I care to remember—and he meant more to me than I think he knew. The past two years had been hard on him and his family, and the pain and stress showed.

He gave a deep sigh. "I hope you know that I respect what you've done with the company."

"Thank you."

"And I don't mean to intrude or interfere."

I tapped my fingers against the desk. "Tell me what you need, Arthur."

"It's about Ada."

I tensed, immediately wary. I had interacted with his daughter only a few times at functions and charity events, had posed for a few photos for the company's sake with them all. The perfect family, the beautiful Hathaways. I couldn't say we'd ever spoken for long, but I knew her well enough to say I didn't like her.

Not in the least.

Spoiled, beautiful and self-centered, she had never once let me forget that I had been her father's lackey at first. Privilege oozed out of every pore—not the type her father had worked his entire life to acquire, but the one that came with the effortless achievement of having been born.

Yeah. I did not like Ada Hathaway.

"What about her?"

"I want to find her a position in the company. No, wait, before you object," Arthur said with a raised hand. "I can see the look on your face. I mean as an intern. She graduated top of her class at Yale, and you know she's intelligent."

I didn't, exactly, but nodded as if that was a given. "Of course, but Arthur, she has very little experience in terms of auctioneering, not to mention business or marketing."

"She completed a summer internship for *Architectural Digest* during her senior year," he argued. "Had nothing but glowing reviews."

I didn't bring up the string of paparazzi photos or the mentions in the tabloids she'd racketed up since then, the many late nights when her father had been called to come and pick her up at one place or another by police or security.

Her exploits had become as famous as she had. I could understand why Arthur was desperate.

"I'm not sure Hathaway's will be a good fit for her," I said honestly.

Seeing the despair in his eyes, I felt nothing but distaste for Ada. Didn't she realize she was breaking his heart with this juvenile behavior? He'd gone through enough.

"All right, Arthur. But if I agree, *if*," I raised a finger in warning, "she needs to show up on time and show respect to the employees. I don't read the tabloids, but I'm not blind."

Arthur's jaw worked, and I saw the frustration and temper in his eyes. Not at me, but at the spoiled creature he was related to.

"Of course. And I would be a phone call away the entire time."

"Have you spoken to her about this? What does Ada say?"

"She's excited at the prospect."

I resisted the urge to snort. I didn't believe that for a second, having seen her pay only a marginal interest in her father's business over the years.

"I'm sure we can find a place for her. Perhaps Greek Artifacts? Or the Oriental division down on Madison and 62nd?" I'd do anything to get her as far away as possible from the headquarters and out of my way.

Arthur shook his head. "I would ideally want her here, next to you. An internship as your assistant perhaps?"

It was a ludicrous suggestion. I would *hate* having to spend months tethered to the hip of a socialite who owed everything to her last name. I only did that on occasion, and then only for one night—when we could both leave the next morning.

But this time? I wouldn't even get sex out of the deal.

"I have a secretary. Linda. She is very good at her job."

"I know. She was once mine," Arthur said with a small smile. "But I'm sure there are things she could hand over to Ada, and things you need done."

I shifted in my seat, intensely uncomfortable. There was no way Ada could be here, with me, for weeks on end. It would not only hinder the effectiveness of my unit but make working here more difficult.

And I'd be damned if I gave the founder's daughter a cushy time, even for Arthur's sake.

"I don't—"

"Please." Arthur leaned forward. "At least consider it. I'm

not asking you to give her special treatment. She needs to perform according to your specifications, of course. And you have the right to fire her if she misbehaves or steps out of line. Don't go easy on her because she's my daughter, all right? All I'm asking is that you give her a foot in the door."

It wasn't too much to ask, in lieu of everything Arthur had done for me. He'd once given me a foot in the door, and now I was the CEO of the company he had spent his life building. Guilt, acidic and annoying, rose up in me.

I opened my mouth to offer up one final argument, but he cut me off.

"Before you say no, Grant, think on it for a day. Let Ada and me attend the company's New Year's social tonight and decide for yourself. She's ready to begin on Monday if you agree."

I pushed a silver pen back in place on my desk, avoiding the plea in his eyes. "Of course, Arthur. I'll see you both there tonight."

"Yes. And thank you again for considering it, truly, Grant. It's always a joy to see what you've done with the place. I know she'll see that too."

I doubted that, but I gave him a short smile. We shook hands and he left with a cheery wave. I leaned back in my chair and dimly heard him making small talk with Linda outside my office. This day had gone from great to terrible in the span of five minutes. I felt as if he had put a great burden at my door, one there was no chance of escaping from.

I had about seven hours to figure out a way.

———

"Mr. Wood. Having a good evening?"

I nodded to the coat check and headed into the event hall Hathaway's usually rented for these company parties. Small, but important in boosting morale—a common feature in the company's history.

I tugged at the sleeve of my suit. I knew what my role was at events like this. Be seen, shake hands, make small talk with as many employees as possible. Listen patiently to breathless pitches and be asked to give my opinion.

And then to leave, so the others could relax and the actual party could start. People wanted the CEO there until it was time to dance and flirt and drink.

Although tonight, I'd have Ada Hathaway to contend with.

Marc, the head of marketing, sidled up to me. "New year, new events."

I nodded and took a flute of champagne from a passing waiter. "Indeed."

"Did you have a nice New Year's Eve?"

"Yes. There's really nothing special about it, is there?"

Marc gave me a sideways grin. "Can't say I agree. We partied in style."

"I can only imagine," I said with a snort. No doubt Marc and his partner had thrown one for the ages. I'd spent the evening at a hotel with skyline view, a hot tub and a date. Forty-two-ounce steak and pepper sauce. It had been fine.

"Oh, look! Arthur's here, and he's not alone." Marc's incredulity was clear. I followed his line of vision to the two people rapidly advancing.

One, the gray-haired former CEO and still a significant shareholder, Arthur Hathaway.

The other, his long-legged, blonde nightmare of a daughter, Ada. It had been a long time since I'd seen her last, nearly half a year, and she was just as effortlessly sensual as always. Seeing her made my stomach clench, my muscles lock down —a physical instinct. I couldn't deny her beauty, like that of a deadly insect or a toxic flower. Warning me to stay away.

She gave me an angelic smile as they stopped before us.

"Arthur! It's great to see you here," Marc said as the two of them shook hands.

"Likewise. It's been far too long."

The two began to talk and Ada turned to me with a raised eyebrow.

I narrowed my eyes at her. "Ada."

"Grant." Her voice was sweet. "It's *lovely* to see you again."

"Likewise."

"How about we leave the kids to it?" Arthur said and put a hand on Marc's shoulder. "I want to hear all about the new apartment."

"You heard about that?"

"Of course…" Their voices trailed off, and alone we were, eyeing one another.

"Kids, huh?" Ada said. "Must have been a long time since someone called you that, Grant."

I forced my jaw to unclench. I couldn't blame Arthur for slipping in his language, even if it was in front of my employees. "It was. I understand you get it daily?"

Her eyes flashed, just slightly, enough to remind me why we usually avoided each other. Nothing good came from our interactions.

She ignored my comment. "Happy New Year, Grant. I'm sure you had a great New Year's Eve?"

"I did." I took a sip of my champagne and looked down at her. Eyes as blue as ice stared coolly back. The punchline was yet to come, I wagered.

"I'm guessing you spent it going through Excel charts, checking off last year's accomplishments and setting next year's?"

"Of course," I said calmly. "How about you? Were you even conscious during the ball drop?"

Ada laughed darkly and looked away. "Let's not fight."

"I thought that was what we did best?" And my hair would go gray if I'd have to deal with it daily for the coming months. Arthur was desperate and delusional—there was no way I could accept his daughter as an intern.

Ada moved in closer and a whiff of her perfume hit me.

Expensive floral notes, mingled with her own scent. My body reacted instinctively and I cursed it for finding her so desirable. *Off-limits, Grant.*

"It is. But can you imagine how much fun we'll have going at it for three months?"

I took a fortifying sip of champagne. "You'd have to live up to my expectations."

"Is that humanly possible?"

"My other employees manage. You'll be like any other intern, Ada. No special treatment."

"I'm not requesting any. I have my own merits." Her eyes were blue steel, gazing into mine, as she unconsciously flicked blonde curls over her shoulder. "You'll see."

A challenge. "Well, I'll enjoy watching you try."

Our staring contest was interrupted by the in-house photographer, a stressed young man who I might like if it wasn't for his ruthless insistence on ensuring the marketing team *always* got the best photos.

It often put us at odds.

"Mr. Wood! Miss Hathaway! Can I get a photo of the two of you? Perhaps with the senior Mr. Hathaway as well?"

I sighed. "Where do you want us?"

"Against the white wall, with the logo. Yes, like that. Give me a moment to ask Mr. Hathaway—stay there, sir!"

Ada leaned against the wall next to me, her long dress billowing out around her like water. She looked fluid, gorgeous, a woman made to be swept up by strong arms. But the smile she shot me was all sharp edges.

"How's my dad?"

"What?"

"I suspect he spends more time lunching and golfing with you than he does with me." Her head tilted slightly to the side. "How's he been?"

Was she truly asking this? I turned to face her entirely. "Not well. It's been two years, but that's no time. It hasn't helped that he's had to worry about you."

Her gaze slid off me and into the distance, heavy lashes lowering. "Are behavioral lectures included in the internship? Or is this just a bonus session?"

"Would you still want it if they were?"

Her focus snapped back to me. "Yes. I'm up to the challenge."

The silent question hung in the air. *Are you?*

"I'm here! Didn't mean to keep you waiting." Arthur hurried to us, an apologetic shrug to his shoulders. I wondered if he'd have apologized three years ago, or ten. The man he'd become after his son died was so radically different. I felt a sudden hatred for Ada then, for not seeing that.

He stepped up beside me. Ada flowed into place on my right, close enough that I felt the warmth from her lithe body.

"All together now!" the photographer called.

Ada's hand slipped under my arm, an intimate movement that brought us closer, made us look like a united front.

"Don't forget to smile, Grant," she murmured to me.

I gritted my teeth.

"Three, two, one…" The flash went off, blinding us all for a moment.

And then she was off, thanking the photographer with a blinding smile and weaving through the crowd. I watched her go. Ada Hathaway, blonde, spoiled, and entirely too snarky for her own good.

"She's welcome to start on Monday," I told Arthur beside me. "A three-month-long internship with the executive unit."

My former mentor gave me a grateful smile. "Thank you. Did she manage to convince you? She can be persuasive."

Hah. "Yes. She did."

Once, years ago, I'd been seated behind her and her twin brother. I had only been working at Hathaway's for a few months and was eager to prove myself.

This was a business I knew I could thrive in, grow, and learn constantly. I could gain the respect of my peers and perhaps one day turn Hathaway's into a full-fledged empire, dealing with real estate, antiques, paintings—everything. I was already wealthy by that point, but I wanted more—I wanted to be untouchable. Filthy rich. Secure.

Ada had been a teenager, rosy and vapid, her hair gleaming before me. Her twin brother had walked as if wearing a halo, the golden son. They carried themselves with that natural grace so much of the Manhattan elite has, their silver spoons practically visible.

Neither of them had seen me seated behind them.

"Have you seen father's new hire?" Max had whispered, loud enough for me to hear.

"Yes," she'd replied. "Pathetic. It's so ironic he's named Grant."

"Follows Father around like a dog," Max had snickered.

I disliked her from the first time I met her, but I truly detested them both that day and vowed to stay as far away from Arthur's children as possible. It hadn't been difficult. They had rarely come by the firm, and when I gradually began to take over from Arthur, I knew that was a closed chapter.

Or it had been, until one of them would start fucking *interning* here.

But... if Ada was here, under my command, she'd have to heed me. I didn't think she'd ever taken orders in her pretty, manicured little life. Perhaps this could even be fun, tormenting her at her own expense. And what had Arthur said earlier?

Don't go easy on her.

I smiled, watching the gold of her hair as she weaved her way effortlessly through the crowd.

I wouldn't.

3

ADA

To my father's credit, I had gotten dressed in a tight pencil skirt, a silk blouse, and my best nude pumps.

And I was there at 7:50 AM, with ten minutes to spare.

In all fairness, I couldn't very well torment Grant if I was fired on the spot. And while I did look forward to potentially being a menace for both Grant and my father, I didn't want the latter to remove me from the trust fund. There was still enough self-preservation in me to see that possibility for the cliff-edge it was.

"I'm Ada," I said to the receptionist when I arrived. "I think Grant Wood might be expecting me?"

She looked up at me with curious eyes, taking in my form. "Do you have an appointment, miss?"

"I do, of a sort. I'm his new intern." I gave her a bright smile. She looked doubtful, and I really couldn't blame her. I felt the same. "It's a new thing," I added. "He might not have informed you."

"Let me call ahead—what did you say your last name was?"

"Hathaway," I said, somewhat uncomfortably. The name was emblazoned in golden letters on the wall behind her desk. "Ada Hathaway."

She put the phone back down. "I'm sorry, Miss Hathaway. Of course. Please take this temporary access card, which will allow you to pass through the gates and get to the relevant floors. Mr. Wood's offices and staff are on the twelfth floor. Just this way. We'll make sure you get a permanent access card later today if you come by security and administration."

"I'll do that, thank you."

She gave me a small nod and an awkward bow, which only made me more uncomfortable.

I straightened my skirt in the elevator. My stomach was in knots, nerves chasing one another. I hadn't actually expected to be nervous about this—I wasn't here to take it seriously—but there was something unsettling in walking into a place where everyone knows *about* you. And likely, most of what they knew was entirely uncomplimentary. And possibly quite untrue.

"Hello dear!" Linda was up and out of her chair before I exited the elevator completely. Her hair had far more gray in it than it did last I saw her, which must have been— Ah, of course. At Max's funeral.

"Hi," I said and returned her hug.

"It's been a long time, sweetheart."

"It has. Is everything all right with you?"

"Yes. Benny has retired now, and he's begging me to do the same. But I could never see myself leaving this place."

I smiled at her. She was as instrumental to this place as the very roof above it. "Of course not. Hathaway's would likely collapse if you did."

"How are you? With everything?"

I gave her a measured nod and the slight half-shrug I had perfected over the many questions from well-wishers and gossips. "Getting better. One step at a time, as they say."

Linda gave a nod and clasped me on the shoulder. "Yes, that is—"

"Ladies." Grant's voice cut through the warm atmosphere in the hallway, his gaze snagging at the half-hug Linda still had me in. "If you're quite done, I have need of you in my office, Miss Hathaway. Let's discuss the terms of your internship."

I smiled apologetically to Linda. "The boss calls."

She winked at me, and returned to her desk as I followed Grant into his office. Grant was a tall, stiff figure before me, clad in an expensive navy suit. It had to be years since I'd last seen him in these rooms.

He looked at home in the office, re-decorated from when it had once been my father's. A new Persian carpet stretched out over a stone floor and a new oak desk sat in front of tall windows.

Grant took a seat and gazed at me with unflinching eyes. I looked back at him with resolve. There was no way I was going to show him that he could intimidate me.

"Let's not beat around the bush. I'm guessing your father convinced you to take this internship."

I flashed a wide smile. "Why, you don't think I'm here to enjoy your sunny company?"

Grant raised an eyebrow, and I hated him for being able to do that and look handsome while doing so. "Shall we pretend that you actually have an interest in this company?"

"It's in my blood," I replied, cocking my head to the side. And it would have passed on to Max someday, perhaps, seeing as he actually enjoyed it. But here was Grant, older and looking decidedly *at home* in this office. Alive and eager. "Why would you assume I don't care?"

"I read the papers, too. Working here will be quite a change of pace from your normal pastimes."

"Maybe having me here will give the firm some star power."

"It has enough on its own," he answered curtly. "You are to be here at eight every morning. You'll participate in the daily brief of events the executive staff runs through. This branch handles the highly delicate items, connections with our most trusted clients, and navigates relations between the different departments. Everyone reports back here. Now, for your first day, I want you to write two-hundred-word reports on every department of Hathaway's and what they specialize in."

"You want me to spend the whole day doing that?"

Grant narrowed his eyes at me, looking infuriatingly superior. "Do you think you're capable of doing that?"

"Yes." I thought I would be done long before the end of the day, but that was another matter.

"Linda will handle all of the practicalities."

"What will be my responsibilities while I'm here?"

Grant gave a small, dismissive wave. "I'll see if I can figure out something. We'll give it some time."

I felt the polite smile freeze on my face. Of course he thought I could do little. Well, perhaps part one of operation annoy Grant would be to prove him wrong. He was like cardboard or steel, stiff and unyielding, a man entirely devoid of sentimental emotions. Max and I had never understood why Father hired him. Or perhaps we had understood it too well —they were entirely alike.

I paused by the door and looked back at him. He cut a stark figure behind the wide desk. Grant had always been tall and lanky, but somewhere in the last couple of years, he had filled out. He must be past thirty now and it showed in the broad sweep of shoulders and strong neck.

"Anything else you need, boss?"

I saw that he picked up on the sardonic lilt I spun on the word *boss*. "No," he said. "Linda will show you to your desk and other administrative details. I'll check in with you at the end of the day, to see how far you've gotten on the overviews."

I shut the door harder than necessary behind me. What a throwaway, imbecilic task. He'd never use the information I compiled in any way. It was just a test.

Linda showed me to my desk, sitting in an open cubicle together with four others.

"These make up the rest of the executive staff, assisting Mr. Wood and this division."

"I'm Adam," a man said and shook my hand. He looked only a little bit older than me, with sandy hair.

"Hi Ada! I'm Sarah." I smiled at the young brunette's exuberance. I'd expected some hesitation or dislike, but they seemed like really nice people.

"That's Michaela's spot. She's not here at the moment but will be returning in the afternoon, so you'll meet her then. She's in charge of communication amongst the different divisions. Come, let's get you all cleared with security."

That alone took nearly an hour. Hathaway's had extensive vaults under the building and 24/7 security guards due to the amount of high-value items stored here at all times, passing through on their way to auction and new owners.

My keycard was encoded and chipped with my photo on it, and I had to memorize an eight-digit code to accompany it.

"Has Mr. Wood given you a task for today?" Linda asked me when I finally returned to my desk.

I nodded. "He has, though it's not very challenging."

"Not for you, of course, dear." Linda smiled. "Glad to see you're all set."

I spun around in my office chair and took a deep breath. This was it, then. I was actually here, at Hathaway's, to work. The whole thing felt entirely surreal.

"What's your task for today?" Sarah asked me. I'd since learned that she was in charge of client relations for the executive branch.

"I'm writing one-page overviews of each and every division in the company."

"Oh. What, why for?" Adam asked.

"For Grant," I replied dryly.

They exchanged glances. "Well, I'm sure it's important then," Adam said carefully.

"I'm fairly sure it's not. But I'll make sure it's done perfectly."

It was just after three PM when I knocked on Grant's door. He'd just returned from a long lunch with a client, and I'd found myself sitting at my desk, straining to see when he returned to his office. It was a habit I'd have to kick—I would *not* spend these months trying to see more of him than I had to.

"Yes?"

He was standing by one of the long bookshelves that covered the far right wall of his office.

"How was lunch?" I asked. "Did you enjoy being wined and dined?"

"I think you'll find that we're the ones who wine and dine the clients. What do you need, Ada?"

I put the thick manila folder on his desk. It hit with a satisfying thud. "I've finished with my little assignment."

His eyes lit up—anticipation. Grant crossed the room in quick strides and grabbed my papers, flipping through them. A frown marked his forehead when he reached the end. Disappointment. He'd wanted me to fail, then. Expected it even.

Miserable man.

"Who assisted you?"

"Nobody. I prepared it myself."

"Hathaway's has thirty-eight divisions. The amount of research this should have taken you—"

"My father worked here for forty-nine years, Grant," I interrupted. "My grandfather spent thirty years building this auction house before that. I'd have to be deaf not to know *something* about it."

He looked at me through narrowed eyes, a hand still holding the folder.

I took a step closer. "So now that you have this super important task completed, what are you going to do with the written overviews?"

"It was a task set for your benefit. I have no use for these."

I took another step closer until I could see the hazel flecks in his eyes. "You really know how to make a woman feel valued, don't you?"

There was a sharp knock on the door. "Sir? I have the information you asked for."

Grant dragged his gaze away from mine with an irritated huff. "Yes?"

A woman with a brown ponytail and heavy eyeliner stepped inside. She stopped in her tracks when she saw us.

"Ada, meet Michaela. Michaela, meet Ada," Grant declared.

"A pleasure," I added. Michaela had regained her composure and now gazed at me with barely disguised distaste. I guessed not everyone in the executive branch had been on board with my sudden addition as an intern.

"Here, sir. The information you wanted. I'd particularly take a look at page twenty-five, where I've highlighted—"

"Yes, thank you, Michaela. Good work."

She turned and left, throwing us one last glance before shutting the door behind us.

"Frosty," I remarked.

Grant looked up from his perusal of the documents. "What?"

"Nothing. What do you want me to do now?" I took a seat on the edge of his desk as I asked it, doing my very best to look irreverent. It was bad enough that he knew I had been forced, like an unruly teen, into being here. I wouldn't give him the satisfaction of being a bad intern, too.

His composure didn't falter, even if he did glance meaningfully at the way I was seated.

"I have things to do. I want you to assist Sarah and Adam with client relations. They'll be able to show you the ropes."

"All right," I said. I assumed I'd passed the test, then.

4

GRANT

It was only day one, but it was becoming crystal clear that the coming months would be the most unproductive I'd ever had.

Ada's smirk when she waltzed in with the finished reports haunted me. I'd have to ask Linda later if Ada had actually done them by herself. I wouldn't put it past her to aim that blinding smile at a junior associate to get a shortcut.

A lamp on my answering machine blinked, and I picked it up to listen to the message, only to put it down with a groan a minute later.

Victoria wanted to head upstate for the weekend. I'd have to call her back and give her the unsatisfying news that I wanted to end things between us.

It wasn't personal.

I just never let things progress to real relationships. It was something I was always clear about from the start—what I wanted and what I was willing to offer. A mutually beneficial arrangement.

But getting closer than that... Letting someone in meant expectations and having to talk about things like feelings and the past and pain, and that was a door I had shut at age fifteen and learned to keep locked ever since.

It wasn't like Victoria would mind. She mostly just enjoyed being on my arm at some of the events I had to go to for business, and I had enjoyed bringing her. But there was nothing more to be done for that.

I opened the stack of documents Michaela had brought and began to read. A new client wanted to list with us—he was considering selling nearly the entirety of his collection of classical artifacts.

All that was left was convincing him.

I spent the rest of the afternoon working and answering phone calls from the heads of divisions. To my own great frustration, curiosity nagged within me to go out and check on how the team was getting on with Ada. I had been determined to ignore her presence and set strict guidelines, and hovering over her shoulder like a fool wouldn't accomplish either.

Adam knocked on my door a little after six in the evening. "I have been showing Ada the ropes on client management," he said. "And she had some great insights about the Burch account."

Damn. *Et tu*, Adam?

I sighed and waved him in. The account was potentially a huge sale and having it take place at our auction house would not only give us a significant commission, but considerable press coverage and notoriety. It couldn't go to our competitors.

"Apparently she used to go to school with Burch's son."

And of course she had. I forced out a small, annoyed sigh. "It's unlikely her connection with his child is going to land us this account."

"You're right, sir," Adam said excitedly, moving forward. "But she knows the old man a little as well. And since you're going to meet him on Thursday, bringing Ada Hathaway along might help seal the deal, so to speak."

"Was this her idea?"

He looked slightly sheepish. "Yes, but I support it. Sarah thought it was a good suggestion as well."

They'd really ganged up on me on this one. And the absolute worst part was that they might be right. Being able to list Burch's collection of Greek and Roman artifacts would be hugely beneficial to the firm. Hathaway's auctions routinely attracted the world's wealthiest collectors, private museums and trusts.

"Thank you, Adam. Send her in?"

Ada walked into my office not two minutes later, her blonde hair perfectly curled behind her ears. She sauntered over to the chair opposite my desk and took a seat, slowly crossing her legs as she did.

I hated that she moved like she owned this place, like she'd been here all of her life.

I hated that she had.

She blinked at me with long, dark lashes. "Yes, Grant? What do you need from me?"

Hell, she was making me say it. "Adam spoke to me of your suggestion. He implied that you have some familiarity with the Burch family."

"Familiarity? Yes. I was in the same school class as Trip for nearly six years. We got on famously."

Trip. I had lived on the Upper East Side for nearly eight years now and still found it hard to stomach some of the old money's stupid-ass nicknames. If I ever met another Chip or Pippa or Finn or Muffy in my life it would be one too many.

"And did you also get on famously with Trip's father, by any chance?"

She gave a low laugh and tossed her hair back over her shoulder. "We've met, yes. Why, you make it sound so lurid!"

I'd only asked a simple question. She was the one behaving atrociously. "I'm driving to Connecticut to meet him and inspect the collection on Thursday."

"And convince him to choose Hathaway's."

"Yes," I said. "As far as I know he hasn't met with another

auction house yet, but he's made it clear that he's looking to sell and the vultures are circling."

"And we want to be the most scavenger-y of the scavengers. Got it."

I narrowed my eyes at her. "Considering your background, your assistance in this meeting might be of value. Do you think you could handle it? I'd run negotiations and the majority of the conversation, of course."

"I know I can," she said primly. "I think I proved today that I know this business well. I have a good way with people, despite what you might think, and I believe Charles will be glad to see me."

I heard the argument she didn't add, clear as day between us. *And I'm a Hathaway.* Her mere presence there would ground the meeting, despite the fact that I had made sure Hathaway's had grown far beyond its Manhattan roots. We had opened offices in twenty-seven new countries since I took over the helm from Arthur.

"The meeting is on Thursday; he's agreed to meet me at his house. We leave at ten in the morning from the office. Dress appropriately, and I want you researching the entirety of his collection tomorrow and everything else you might need to convince him."

"Give Trip a call, you mean?" she asked dryly. "Remind him of our friendship?"

I half-shrugged. "Like one of his photos on some social media platform, what do I know."

"Poke him on Facebook?"

"What?"

"Never mind." She shook her head with a small smile that made it clear she'd been mocking me in some capacity or another. God, she exemplified perfectly why I should stop dallying with girls from this area for good. "Do you want me to order a car for us?"

"No, I'll drive us."

Her eyes widened slightly, giving me instant satisfaction. "People do still drive their own cars, you know."

Ada pursed her lips in irritation. "Thanks for the update. I simply didn't think the great Grant Wood, CEO of Hathaway's, deigned to do that sort of thing. Productivity 101, and all that. Can't very well reply to emails if you're behind the wheel."

That was one of the things I had weighed in the balance when I decided not to use a car service, and it annoyed me that she'd zeroed in on it so quickly. "I like driving," I said simply. "Now, you have research to do."

The door closed behind her and I released a pent-up breath. Something about Ada managed to slip right underneath my skin, like a splinter under a nail. No one else in this company would dare call me Grant, and most definitely not an intern or any of the trainees the other divisions regularly hosted.

I could see it in her eyes, the laughing disrespect. But what annoyed me the most?

With her, it *bothered* me.

5

ADA

The others at the office were both helpful and positive about the upcoming trip—with one notable exception. Michaela said nothing at all to me, leaving for a meeting with a comment to Sarah that *it isn't right that interns were given such privileges, particularly with clients of this magnitude.*

It hurt, mostly because it was true.

I had spent the entire previous day growing accustomed to the job and learning everything there was to know about Charles Burch's collection. The individual pieces had varying amounts of information available, but I memorized it all.

Grant came out of his office just before ten. He wore a three-piece gray suit, and his hair was thick and dark as it fell over his brow. It pained me to admit—even to myself—just how handsome he was. If only he knew how to smile, he might just be attractive.

"Let's go," he said, barely even shooting me a glance.

"Good luck," Sarah whispered as I gathered up my files and my handbag. I winked at her as I followed Grant out to the elevator.

"Good," he said, glancing down at the documents I had in my hand. "You can use the drive to go over the details again."

"I did that yesterday. I know them already."

He raised an eyebrow, as if he doubted this, so I gave him a sweet smile. "And are these clothes to your liking?"

Grant turned to me fully. "What?"

"You told me to dress appropriately."

His gaze traveled down my tailored dress in navy, which reached to just above my knee. I looked entirely professional and entirely plain, much, I thought snidely, like him.

Grant gave a short nod. "Yes. Terrific."

We walked in silence through the garage, finally arriving at the square reserved for the company's CEO. Grant's car was a classic BMW, black with tinted windows. "This is a nice car," I said. "It shows a lot of personality."

"Thanks," he replied. I didn't even think he caught the sarcasm.

A two-hour drive with Grant Wood. And only four days earlier I had been with friends and their friends, surrounded by carefree laughter and easy ways to escape. How quickly life could change.

Grant's hands were wide and comfortable on the wheel. He didn't wear a wedding band, and I realized that I didn't actually know a lot about him. Not that there was likely much to know, I thought dryly, considering the way he had lived for work since my father first hired him.

"Where did you go to university?" I asked him, trying to think back to what I'd heard. Not a whole lot, really. One minute he had been Dad's mentee, present everywhere he was.

Grant's hands seemed to tighten around the steering wheel. "We're not here to exchange pleasant chitchat," he said. "We work together, and we will remain professional."

"Despite our private history?"

"Our what?"

"Your close relationship with my father? The fact that I've known you for what, six years?"

"We haven't really known each other," he said in an icy voice. "We've just met on occasion."

"Then let's remedy that. Where are you from?"

"What do you mean?"

"Where were you born?" I said slowly. God, this man really was difficult. A cardboard cutout of a human, having to be taught basic human behavior. I wondered if he had an *off* button, or perhaps *reset*.

"In New York," he replied.

"The city? The state?"

"State."

"It's a large state."

He shrugged. "Upstate." His tone made it clear he was done with this line of conversation, and I silently cheered. I'd managed to make a nuisance out of myself.

"A big family? Do you have legions of siblings running around?"

"No."

"Was your goal always to become the head of an international auction firm when you were a little boy?"

"Was your goal always to become a drifting socialite when you were a little girl?"

I narrowed my eyes at him. Unprofessional, indeed. "As a matter of fact, yes. Some people had posters of bands and actors; mine were of derailed child celebrities and New York heiresses."

Almost despite himself, his lip curled. "Glad you can see it that way."

The silence stretched on between us. I fiddled with the hem of my dress and watched the landscape pass by outside.

"So," I said finally, determined to break the silence he so wanted to keep. "Does my father often berate you into accepting interns? Or am I just a lucky exception?"

"No. Arthur seldom comes into the office anymore," Grant replied. I curled my hand against my side. So much for lighthearted conversation.

"It's been difficult for him since Max," Grant added. "But—"

"I know. I would rather not talk about that." I busied myself with rearranging the seat belt. Of course he had to take this conversation to a new low by mentioning my brother. I'd asked questions about his family; he retaliated in kind.

"As you wish," he said. "Now tell me what you've remembered about Burch's collection."

We spent the rest of the drive rehashing the strategies for the visit and the details of the collection. We pulled up along a large, tree-lined street in New Haven, snow dusting the road. Iron gates greeted us and Grant lowered his window.

"Mr. Wood and Miss Hathaway here from Hathaway's to meet with Charles Burch," he said to the electronic speaker.

"Come on in," a voice replied, distorted by the radio.

The gates swung open and Grant drove us into the wide front yard and around a beautiful fountain, frozen in the cold.

"They've repainted the house," I remarked. "It used to be blue, not gray."

Grant gave me a sideways glance. "You didn't tell me you'd been here before."

I smiled at him. "Whoops."

We walked up the portico just as Charles opened the front door. "Welcome! It's a pleasure to have you here. Ada, you look as lovely as ever." He bent to give me a hug, and I responded with a wide grin. I hadn't seen him for almost five years, but there was a time I had visited nearly weekly.

"Hi, Mr. Burch. How have you been?"

He looked well, if a bit more gray-haired than I remembered him. "Great. I have thought of you often, my dear, and your father with you."

"Thank you," I said. "That means a lot to us."

Charles turned to Grant, who looked slightly annoyed at not having been greeted first.

"Mr. Wood. It's a pleasure to meet you."

"Likewise, Mr. Burch. I've been looking forward to viewing your collection for ages."

29

Charles gave a proud smile. That was one of the things I had always loved about Trip's eccentric, bookish father—he was genuinely kind.

"You must be especially eager to see the Phidias piece?"

"Yes, I am. But also the one by Scopas. Such a rare piece."

Charles looked over at Grant with raised eyebrows, as if seeing him for the first time. "Indeed. It's the lesser known of the two, naturally, but knowing the history behind the artifact and its creator, its undeniably the more magnetic."

I struggled to hide a smile as I followed the two of them through the foyer and into the wide sunroom where the collection was housed.

The two of them moved up the length of the room, pausing at each old stone sculpture artfully placed and lighted within glass boxes. It was a small collection, but valuable—each piece had been tracked down and bought at auctions around the world. I knew it was Charles's lifework, and his passion for the art was clear in the warmth in his voice when he described each piece to Grant and me.

It had been a long time since I had been a small girl occasionally accompanying my dad for consultations, or being shown around the Hathaway's vault by one of the security guards. If Hank worked when we were there, he would take Max and me in each hand when we had nothing to do but wait. *This is a beautiful piece*, he'd say, peering over at a painting or a blue-and-white Chinese vase. And then he'd make up some marvelous story about its origins involving pirates or fairies and genies and we'd giggle and ask for more. *What about this one, Hank? Where did this one come from?*

The feeling of marvel was one I hadn't felt in a long time, and seeing it so clearly on both Grant's and Charles's faces sparked a corresponding ache inside.

"Now take a look at this piece," Charles said finally, stopping at the centerpiece. It was the only one we hadn't yet discussed, and I didn't recognize it from the information we had studied the day prior.

"This is new?"

Charles nodded. "About a year since I bought it. It was the final piece I sought to crown the collection."

Grant stood silently, taking in the large, naked woman on the plinth. She lacked an arm and a head, the wide torso clad in a tunic and a shield clasped in her remaining hand. The marble work was beautiful.

"Artemis?" I suggested. "Or Diana, depending on whether it's Roman or Greek."

"Has to be Greek," Grant said, leaning closer to observe the detailed work on the shield. "200 BC?"

Charles gives an impressed nod. "Yes, it's a statue of Artemis from 300-200 BC, from one of the Greek isles. It came to me entirely legally, but suffice it to say that I find this collection worthy of a larger audience."

"Yes, it's truly stunning," Grant said. "And on that note, shall we discuss your objectives and hopes with a possible auction?"

"I want to sell the collection in its entirety."

"Are you certain?" I asked. Since I heard about it I'd been surprised at his desire to part with something he'd spent decades researching, searching for, and loving.

I could see Grant in my peripheral view as he turned to me with incredulity, but I ignored him.

Charles nodded at me, kindness in his eyes. "It's time. I have never seen myself as their owner, anyways, merely a steward on their eternal path. And I want them to be sold with museums and art collections in mind. Where is no matter, only with the stipulation that they must be displayed on occasion for public view."

"We can do that." Grant nodded. "I agree with you; they should be enjoyed by the many."

Charles gave a sudden, wide smile. It looked as if a weight had been lifted off his shoulders. "Then it's settled."

"When would you want it to take place?"

"Whenever you think it best."

"Mid-February," Grant offered. "Gives us time to properly photograph each item and get the information out to relevant media outlets and interested museums."

"Our lawyers can handle the rest, I assume?"

Grant nodded. "Yes. And I'm of course always available, should you have any questions."

"Great. That's great. And Ada, I'm so happy to see you working for your father's company. Interning, was it?"

"Yes, that's it."

"He must be very happy with that."

I thought of the disappointment in his eyes when he told me this was the last chance, the final straw. "Yes," I said. "He's so pleased."

6

GRANT

There wasn't much unplanned about my days. I woke up at the same time each morning, I followed the same exercise routine. I was pretty sure I had used the same shampoo for nearly a decade at this point.

My home followed the same rules. A date I had brought to my apartment a few months back had called it *pristine*. When put that way, I supposed it did lack the personal effects or touches other people cherished. But who had the time for that? Being set in my ways had never steered me wrong in the past, and I saw no reason to change that now.

And in my professional life?

Routine meant cash, and cash was king.

I sat at the head of the conference table, my fingers tapping against the edge of the oak wood.

"Does anyone know where she is?"

Michaela shook her head, her arms crossed over her chest.

"I'm sure she'll be here in a moment," Sarah offered. Adam and Linda exchanged glances.

It was nearly five minutes past eight, and the coming days were going to be hectic for the firm. We had a physical auction a day, as opposed to the frequent online auctions. The physical auctions were hugely important as they gave prospective buyers a chance to see the goods they were buying—not to mention mingle with other buyers, to see and be seen.

"We won't wait for an intern," I said. "The auction today includes both books and manuscripts; we all know this is one that tends to attract large crowds of speculative buyers. Adam, how many registered bidders do we have for today?"

"Nearly 150, with almost 20 more registered to bid over the phone."

"Good. The division for expert—"

"I'm sorry I'm late! So sorry." Ada burst through the door, her golden hair catching the light. She was flushed and with a sickeningly cute movement, she reached up to tuck a stray lock behind her ear.

"I got caught in the elevator with the division head for contemporary art. Couldn't get away, terribly—"

"Sit down," I told her. "Don't be late again."

She fell quiet and shot me an irritated glare. I almost felt a twinge of guilt for my harsh tone, but reminded myself of her own usually acidic rhetoric. Ada took a seat next to Sarah, and I saw the older woman lean in and whisper something in her ear. Adam wasn't just smitten with her, but Sarah too?

Couldn't anyone be on my team?

"We've held many of these auctions before, and this one is no different. There's a first edition of *Jane Eyre* selling today, and they're very rare. It will be the last piece we sell today. You all know your roles."

"What's mine?" Ada asked.

"You'll help Michaela in anything she needs, in organizing the contact with the division for Books and Manuscripts."

Michaela smiled, but Ada didn't return it. I shook my head. Would it kill the girl to show some manners? She had been more than able to with Charles only a couple of days prior. The memory was unsettling. She had known more than I had expected.

And when she interacted with him... It had been a

different person I saw, one that had never been around me before. Kind, and almost… vulnerable. Though that was a word I had never before associated with the Hathaways.

I shook the thought away. I knew exactly who Ada Hathaway was, and wouldn't be fooled by bright smiles and twinkling eyes.

7

ADA

Dad called after lunch. I stepped out of the office and onto the small terrace facing the interior courtyard. It was cold outside and I should have brought a coat, but I was fairly sure the conversation wouldn't last long enough for me to need it.

"How's the job?"

This was the first time he'd checked in since I began. "It's good," I told him. "Interesting. We have a Book and Manuscript auction for today."

"Yes, I saw," he said. Of course. He probably checked Hathaway's website almost daily, a habit he was unlikely ever to lose. "How's Grant as a boss?"

Superior, I wanted to reply. Infuriating. Occasionally smug. Surprisingly competent.

"Good," I said. "He's good."

"I'm glad to hear it."

"It's odd being back here. It's been a long time since—"

"Yes, it certainly has." Dad cleared his throat again. "Well, it's good to hear that you're all right. I'll probably be in town again this weekend. I'll call you for dinner."

"Goodbye, then."

He'd already hung up. Since Max, he spent most of his time in the house in the Hamptons. It was our old Nana's house, but now he used it as his home base. Our family apartment on Park Avenue stood empty. I knew both of us had the keys to it, but there was too much pain in being there. Empty rooms for people who were no longer here. We should have sold Mom's piano right away, I thought. And Max's collection of baseball cards. Maybe then we would have stood a chance.

But I knew it wasn't the things—memories haunted that place.

Michaela grabbed a hold of me when I returned to the office. "Come with me," she said cheerily. "Let's go through the chain of events for today."

She was painstakingly meticulous on the time schedule of the auction, and all the goods that needed to arrive.

"Ensure that this list makes it to the ground team by two o'clock. They'll need it to set up the order of the goods displayed. Do you have any questions?"

I got the vague feeling that I was back in school somehow, but I did my best to think. "What auctioneer are we using today?"

"Roderick."

"When will Grant arrive?"

She frowned. "When he wishes to."

Of course. The comings and goings of such a superior being clearly defied time and space. Everyone's hero worship of him was understandable—I could recognize the expansive growth Hathaway's had undergone under his leadership— but it remained just as tiring.

"I want you to go speak to the Book and Manuscript specialists. Tell them we're not moving the *Jane Eyre* manuscript—it's not to be displayed today. It's a blind bid."

"Why not?" I frowned. The rest of the artifacts were all displayed, per usual. Hathaway's prided itself on the lighting and presentation of each good sold whenever it hosted a physical auction. It was drilled into me, into my very bones.

"The owners haven't given permission for it to be moved, and it's highly sensitive. This is all routine, really, Ada."

She ran off to handle phone calls, and neither Sarah nor Adam were in the office. So I did what I was told, though the specialists down at Book and Manuscript were surprised at my demand. But since I came from Executive, they nodded and shrugged.

Linda spent the afternoon teaching me how to handle Grant's calendar and the company email, sorting through the flood of emails the company gets each day, and allocating them to the right person.

So when I hurried down to the auction floor it had already begun, a flurry of activity and raised paddles. I saw Grant and Adam in the wings, watching.

Adam smiled at me when I arrived. "CNN is here," he whispered. "And several of the key bidders represent both public and private library collections across the world."

"Wow."

Grant looked up from his phone. "Are all the pieces accounted for and ready to be displayed?"

"Yes, except the last one."

His eyes narrowed suddenly with a razor-sharp focus as they snapped to mine. "*Except* the last one?"

"Yes. It's still in the Books and Manuscript Department."

"So the first edition *Jane Eyre* isn't here?" Grant spoke slowly. "It's still in preservation?"

I swallowed. "Yes, that's right."

He closed his eyes and took a deep, heavy breath. I hurried to explain myself and the decision I thought was correct. "Because it's a highly sensitive edition, not to be moved without the owner's permission?"

"The owners are selling with us," Grant spoke through gritted teeth. "That means they are trusting us with the guard, keep and preservation of it. They have already given implicit permission when they listed with us."

"Oh." Michaela had been wrong, then. Entirely. Not for the first time, I wondered if she was trying to sabotage me.

"Ada. I understand that this means little to you. I know

you'd rather be in St. Tropez, or at Saks Fifth Avenue. But while you are here, under my command, you will not deliberately undermine my company. You may be useless, but try not to be downright harmful."

I swallowed. My eyes were burning, and I could feel it, the hot rush of shame and anger. This conversation needed to end, now, or I would do something completely unforgivable and mortifying like cry in front of Grant.

Grant looked away from me with a tired sigh. "I suppose I'll just have to try to sell these unseen."

"Can I help?" I asked, because despite what he might think, I didn't want to be a liability. There was a part of me that's always wanted to do the right thing, to be of use, and that part was heartbroken.

Grant shook his head and turned. "No. You've done enough. I need to find Michaela."

I nodded and tried to look dismissive, because I didn't trust my voice enough to speak. I didn't stay to watch the auction. I returned to the executive floor, finding it deserted, with only Linda remaining. She was on the phone, so I sat down at my desk and stared blankly at the screen.

I'd learned three things today.

1. Michaela disliked me and would try to sabotage my internship at Hathaway's.

2. I might have taken this job as a way to ensure access to my trust fund and to annoy Grant, but I genuinely cared for it now. I wanted to do a good job.

3. Grant didn't believe me particularly capable—and that actually *bothered* me.

And of the three, it was the last one that surprised me the most.

8

GRANT

The day passed without issue, with the exception of a knock on my door.

"Hi Linda," I said when she stepped inside. "What's up?"

She took a seat in the chair opposite me, entirely devoid of her usual authoritative manner. This wasn't like her.

"Is something wrong?"

"You have always been a fair boss, and a good one."

I was instantly put on edge, and leaned back, crossing my arms over my chest. "But?"

"It's about Miss Hathaway, sir."

"What about her?"

"She's hard-working and very clever. And I'd hate for a few bad days to make you think anything differently."

Of course. Ada had champions in every corner, beloved immediately because of her smiles and her last name. Why should I have assumed any of these people would show me more loyalty than her?

"She has to prove her worth, same as anyone else in this company."

"I know that, sir. And being late yesterday was on her— even if it was a small lapse, and one we all do from time to time. But I digress," she said, noting the expression on my face. "My concern is rather the auction yesterday."

Ah, how could I forget. When Ada had somehow, brainlessly, decided not to ensure the first edition manuscript made it to the auction floor. "I was informed by Michaela that it was the one thing Ada was put in charge of. It's a mistake, and one she won't do again if she wants to stay here."

"But that's the thing, sir. I don't want to go behind anyone's back, but my loyalty is to you and to the company. And to the truth."

"What is it, Linda?"

"I overheard Michaela telling Ada to go down to the Books and Manuscript division and tell them not to include the first edition *Jane Eyre* in the transfer. It was a direct order. Ada even questioned it."

"That can't be true."

Linda looked pensive, her hand gripping the side of her chair. She had been here nearly forty years and there was no one with more integrity. If she said it, it had to be true—but why? And for what reason?

"I don't think Michaela has taken kindly to Ada's presence on the team."

"What makes you say that?"

"Call it intuition. And while I might be out of bounds on this, sir, has Michaela ever indicated to you that she is interested? Beyond the strictly professional?"

I blinked at her. The notion felt ludicrous. She was an objectively attractive woman, I supposed, but I would never be intimate or encourage it with anyone on my staff.

"Never," I replied. But even so, instances flashed in my memory, of her asking if I wanted her to stay late. Of her offering to bring me coffee, despite it being decidedly out of bounds for her to do so in her position as division head.

"But why would that make her dislike Ada?"

Linda gave an elegant shrug that somehow spoke legions. "I'm not sure, sir. That would be anyone's guess."

41

And she had already made her guess—it was clear in the silence. But the idea of Ada and me as an item of romance was not only impossible, it was comical. *Absolutely not.* I was not a man fit for relationships, and God knew she disliked me plenty. Not to mention the implications of such a liaison on Arthur Hathaway and the fallout when it inevitably went south.

Unbidden, the image of her face when she had arrived late to the meeting, beautifully flushed, came to my mind. I could see it, her flushed like that for other reasons, stretched out atop the linen sheets of my bed.

Impossible. Oddly alluring. And entirely, entirely inappropriate.

Linda continued to stare at me with a peculiar expression, as if she could see all of this and more.

I shook my head as if to clear it. "Thank you, Linda. You have given me much to think about."

"Will you ensure that Ada isn't punished further? It was truly not her mistake."

I gave her a nod. "Leave it up to me."

How I would go about that discussion, I had no idea.

———

I had a twenty-minute window after my meeting with the division for British Paintings, so I called Michaela into my office.

She was silent and serious as she walked in, taking a seat opposite me. She'd worked with us for over six months. And now I'd likely have to train someone else. God, I didn't need this.

"What do you need, sir?"

"I'd like to discuss what happened yesterday, with the *Jane Eyre* manuscript."

Michaela nodded. "It's a pity it was not displayed during the auction. I take part of the blame, of course. I shouldn't have trusted Ada with something of such consequence."

"It's lucky we managed to sell it based on the photos you had on your drive."

"I think the new owners will be pleased."

"And you didn't give Ada explicit orders to inform the Books and Manuscript department that the first edition *not* be moved, because it was—and I quote—sensitive?"

Michaela looked shocked. I had to give it to her, the woman knew how to act, at least. "Why would I have done that? Hathaway's has excellent specialists, of course we could move an item despite its age or fragility."

"Quite right. Unless you did it so that Ada would look bad."

Michaela shook her head. "Sir, these are outlandish accusations. Why would I risk my job like that? Did Ada tell you this herself? Don't believe her lies."

"Her lies," I repeated, nodding along as if I was on the same page.

"Yes. She's been nothing short of a nuisance since she came. Hasn't proven that she belongs here."

"Have you given her a chance to prove it?"

Michaela looked taken aback by my change in demeanor. "Yes. But she hasn't."

"She's been here four days," I said. "And it wasn't Ada who came to me with this. Someone else overheard you give those specific instructions to her."

Michaela's face fell. "That's not possible."

"That you were overheard?"

She shook her head. "Sir, I don't... It was only to show you what we all already knew—she's not a good fit for this company."

"And you took it upon yourself to manipulate events, rather than trust that my judgment would prevail?"

She swallowed. "I made a mistake. I realize that. It won't happen again, sir."

"Quite so, because I want you to pack up your things today and leave Hathaway's."

Her eyes widened. "I've spent years working my way up to this position. I promise it won't happen again. Grant, please…"

If she was trying to appeal to my emotional nature, she was failing hard. "What you did put the company in jeopardy, and risked an ongoing auction. Not only that, but you willingly sabotaged a team member. Both of those things are unforgivable, and I cannot have a member of my staff that I do not trust. I will let you go with a reference—if, and only if, you make it clear to new employers what happened here and that it won't again. But your future at Hathaway's is over."

Michaela left without another word. From the look in her eyes, she was disappointed with me—as if I had been the problem! She packed up her things in silence.

Linda was quiet at her desk. I was glad that Adam, Sarah and Ada were all out of the office at the moment—away on some meeting or another. It made this a whole lot easier.

Michaela stopped in the corridor, her bag in hand. "Mr. Wood, I can't begin to say how sorry I am. I hope that you'll find it in your heart to forgive me."

God, this woman gave herself too much credit. "You're forgiven," I said. "And in a moment, you'll also be forgotten. If you have any further logistical questions regarding the termination of your contract, feel free to contact HR or Linda. Goodbye."

The door fell shut behind her, and a second later I heard the chime of the elevator.

"What a mess," I told Linda, because quite frankly, it was. "When did this branch devolve into a kindergarten?"

She patted me on the shoulder, likely the only person who could get away with it. "Now now, dear. You did what was necessary. And there are plenty of talented junior staff who can fill her position."

I nodded. "I assume there are. Will you tell Ada to come to my office as soon as she can, when she returns?"

"Of course."

I returned to my work but found it nearly impossible to focus. Now I'd have to *apologize*. To Ada Hathaway. And the worst part was, I felt guilty. The things I had said to her were entirely unprofessional and far harsher than I would have, had I not been so angry. Had it not been her there to break the news to me. There was no doubt that I wouldn't have gone off on like that on, say, Adam. I didn't like the effect she had on me.

A soft knock sounded from my door. "Grant?"

"Come in."

One might think it would be difficult for a gorgeous young blonde to look like she wanted to murder you quietly in your sleep, but no. That was exactly what the glare Ada shot me said. And I deserved it.

She sat down before me, looking down at her nails. "I understand if you want to discuss what happened yesterday, but I want you to know that it won't happen again."

"I know it won't. I've fired Michaela."

Pure satisfaction pulsed through me at the shock on Ada's face. Whatever she thought I'd say, it wasn't that.

"You've done what?"

"She was the one who told you the first edition shouldn't be moved, was she not?"

Ada gave a slow nod. "Yes. But I didn't tell you that."

"No. Why not?" This part genuinely intrigued me. "You could have defended yourself with the truth."

"Would you have believed me over Michaela?" Her tone was wry. "No? Didn't think so."

I shifted uncomfortably. The honest answer was that I probably wouldn't have. And that didn't really sit well.

"How'd you find out, anyway?"

"Linda overheard her give you the instruction."

The triumph in Ada's eyes had little to do with the revelation, I thought, and more with the fact that it proved her theory. Without Linda to back her up, I might not have believed her.

"I said some harsh things yesterday that were unwarranted. I want you to know that the work you've done here so far has been surprising."

Ada looked incredulous. "Is this an apology from Grant Wood?"

"Don't push it," I warned her. "I'm going to ask Adam to take over some of Michaela's tasks while we search for a replacement. That means you'll be assisting Sarah on client control. Think you can handle it?"

"Oh, Grant," Ada said, rising with a wide smile. "I'll show you client control."

9

ADA

It was a sunny winter day when I arrived the following week, annoyed and upset, to find that everyone in the executive branch had skipped the eight AM meeting. There was no one in the conference room.

"Hello?" I said to the empty office.

"Ada, is that you? We are in Mr. Wood's office," Linda called.

An unusual tableau greeted me; they were all splayed out around Grant's table, papers and computers everywhere. Adam looked like he hadn't slept, and Sarah had her usually immaculate hair in a flat ponytail.

Grant stood at the helm of the table. "Ada. Come on in."

"What's happening?"

"Jack and Thorn's," Linda sighed, the name of our main competitors echoing through the room. "They outsold us last week. They're putting on an offensive to capture most of the Old Masters market, outselling us on commission fees."

Ah. So this was a war room.

"What are we to do?"

Linda patted the chair next to her and I took a seat. Grant smiled, and it was full of savage promise—he wasn't the youngest and most successful CEO in Hathaway's history for nothing. "We retaliate."

"Can I help? I know we are one short on executive staff. Use me if you need to, anywhere."

I was half expecting a scoff, but Grant only nodded. "We will have need of you. I think it'd be good if you assist the relevant divisions in this, help coordinate the new sellers we need to attract."

"Of course. I also know Ben Harris a little, if you need information on him."

Grant's eyes snapped to mine. "You know the new CEO of Jack and Thorn's?"

I played with the hem of my skirt, slightly uncomfortable with the sudden attention of everyone around the table. Even Adam had put down his pen.

"A little. He's worked there for years before becoming CEO, and I'm a Hathaway." I shrugged. "We usually exchange pleasantries at events and the like."

Grant's focus instantly became laser-like. "What's your take on him?"

"Competitive. Charming. Prefers vodka martinis over those made with gin, which is never a good sign. I'm not sure how much art or cultural experience he has but he doesn't strike me as someone who accepts losing."

"Well, neither am I," Grant said.

We worked intensely that day. All avenues were explored for how to draw more sellers to choose Hathaway's, from drops in commissions to other sellers premiums. The trick with auctioneering was that you had to make people want to sell *and* make people want to buy, all at the same time.

I'd always watched Dad's business from a distance, proud and jealous at once. It had taken him away from us for so many evenings and weekends and school graduations.

But I was starting to see the appeal, too.

———

"Thank you," I said to the delivery guy. "You're a lifesaver."

He gave me a wan smile. "Hear that all the time, beautiful."

The scent of Thai curry filled the elevator on my way back up to the executive floor, making my stomach rumble. It was nearly eight in the evening, and most of the other divisions were entirely empty and dark by now. But not us.

I met Linda on my way out of the elevator. "You're staying, dear?"

I nodded. "A while longer, at least."

"See you tomorrow, then. Oh, that smells good."

"From Pork and Moos," I said. "Best Thai takeout on the Upper East Side."

"Adam just headed out, too. Just you and Mr. Wood left."

"All right."

"Don't stay too late," she said with a wink that I decided not to decipher. Linda had known me since I was a child. She was probably alluding to my former days as a party girl, if anything. But definitely not to anything between me and Grant.

He was still sitting at the large working table in his office, papers spread out before him. His thick hair stood up in disarray as if he'd just been running his hands through it in frustration.

He looked up when I entered. "Food?"

"Even the great Grant Wood can't run without fuel." I began to unpack the boxes as he fastidiously made space for them, moving his precious papers out of distance from any potential food stains.

"Thai?"

"Yes, and some spring rolls. Don't you like it?"

"I do," he replied. "I just didn't think you did."

"What's that supposed to mean?" I laughed.

He shook his head. "Well, it's not foie gras or lobster."

"Hey, I enjoy all types of food. I don't discriminate.

Besides, who are you to talk? I saw you driving an Aston Martin last summer, buddy."

"Yeah, but I didn't grow— Never mind." Grant shook his head. "Thanks for getting the food."

"Of course. My knowledge of all the best takeout places has to come in handy sometimes. Chopsticks?"

"No."

"Why?" I grinned.

"I don't use chopsticks."

I raised an eyebrow. "You've never tried, in other words."

He rolled his eyes. "Yes, that's what I mean. Come on. Don't hold the food hostage."

Grant reached across the table and grabbed one of the boxes. He took a bite of his Pad Thai, and I was momentarily distracted by his lips. I'd never noticed how full they were before, or how long his lashes were. He truly was an attractive man. Not for me—never for me—but I could appreciate beauty where I saw it. After all, I'd been an art major.

"Everyone else has left," he told me. "I don't expect you to have to stay much longer either, you know. It's late."

"And give you another excuse to call me useless? No, I don't think so."

He raised an eyebrow. "I deserved that."

"Besides, the others have a family to get home to." I shrugged. "I don't. I'm guessing you don't either?"

He shook his head, still bent over the noodles. I already suspected that, of course. Grant didn't wear a wedding ring despite the fact that he was often pictured with women in the various magazines in the art and auction world.

There was something so odd about seeing him like this— down to his shirtsleeves, broad shoulders stretched out not in work or in action but to eat, his hair free from its usual neat waves. I shook my head and tried to focus back on my red curry and the fact that I was working late with a man I had despised for so many years. Funny how life works out.

I looked up and saw Grant holding one of Jack and Thorn's latest magazines in a death grip, his fork in his other hand.

"I can't let Hathaway's fail," he said.

"Hang on a moment. Nobody said anything about the company failing? We just have some friendly competition. They still have a smaller market share than us. We'll figure something out."

Grant stared at the Jack and Thorn's logo as if it were the devil and didn't reply, so I reached over and pried the magazine carefully from his hand. "Hey," I said. "What did you do within your first six months at this company?"

Grant looked up at me. "Sorry?"

"You orchestrated the largest single contemporary art sale in modern history."

His lip curled at that. "287 million dollars in one hour."

"You did that within your first year at Hathaway's. You were twenty-four at the time."

Grant's eyes refocused entirely on me. "You've been watching me."

I rolled my eyes. "Of course I have. You're basically all my father has been able to talk about since you started working here."

He snorted. "Right."

"Plus, how many more locations worldwide do we have distributors at now?"

"Forty-seven."

"How many new divisions have been added under your leadership?"

"Eight." His gaze was tinged with amusement. "You know, hearing Ada Hathaway recite a list of my achievements was probably the last thing I thought I'd be doing tonight."

"Funny how things turn out, isn't it?"

He ran a hand through his hair again, and it slid like silk through his fingers. I was momentarily distracted, thinking about how it would feel between my own fingers. How soft it'd be at the nape of his neck.

"I didn't know you'd studied art history until Linda informed me this morning."

"Didn't you ask for my CV before hiring me?" I smiled. "I'm sure we spoke about this at my interview."

He rolled his eyes. "Very funny."

"It's not like I could have studied anything else, is it?" I folded the edges of my empty takeout box and put it back in the plastic bag.

"Do you really feel like that? Obligated?"

I searched for the two fortune cookies, hidden under a mountain of napkins and small packets of soy sauce. "I guess so, a little bit. But I did enjoy it. I think I might like the design aspect more, though—the drawing and painting. Creating."

He accepted the cookie I handed him with a slight frown. "I thought you ordered from a Thai place?"

"They specialize in fusion cuisine," I said with as straight a face as I could manage. "You can get sushi, Chinese and Thai, all from the same menu."

He smiled as he opened the packet. "I don't think I've had one of these in years."

"How have you survived, without the excellent guidance they provide? What does yours say?"

Grant pulled out the small roll of paper. "'Love is as necessary to human beings as food and shelter.' Hah. Well, I remember why I so seldom read these."

"Come on, that's arguably true."

"Sure," he snorted. "What does it say on yours?"

I unrolled the small piece of paper. "'Well-arranged time is the surest sign of a well-arranged mind.'" I hadn't even finished before I heard Grant's laughter. It was deep and rich, and I knew instantly that I would need to hear it again. Find a way to spark it, somehow.

"What?" I reached over and hit him on the arm. It was firm under my touch. "What's so funny with that?"

"Nothing. Just, of all the things you could have gotten... Ada, even you have to find that a bit humorous."

I did. "Well then, Mr. Wood. If I'm in need of a more well-arranged mind, then you're in need of love. Hey, don't pull that face at me. I don't make the rules. The cookies have spoken."

He scoffed and put his own finished takeout box in the bag. "Right. How presumptuous of me to disregard the fortune."

"Give that to me." I took the bag from his hand and tossed it in the trash by the door to his office. On my way back I was struck by the sheer quantity of books he had. They filled the entire far right of his office, leather-bound or colorful. I ran a hand down the spines on one shelf.

Artifacts of Roman Britain

Etruscan Jewelry

The Collected Works of Michelangelo

His office was a veritable library. "How many of these have you actually read?"

Grant looked up at me. "Nearly all," he said, and turned his attention back to the file at hand. He must have felt my silent incredulity, though, because he flicked his attention back to me. "You should try it sometime."

"Being a know-it-all?"

"Reading."

"Very funny."

"It might actually give you a well-arranged mind."

"My teachers at the Yale Department of Art History would salivate at all of this. You could practically teach courses in here."

He snorted. "Right."

"You didn't go to university, did you?" I asked. It was a challenge and a guess, but from the way his eyes snapped to mine, it had to be true. The silence stretched out between us, beats of uncertainty and heat.

"I did other things," he said finally, breaking my gaze. He

flipped through some of the papers faster than I thought he could actually read. "A lot of the people who come in here will lord their degrees or their specialist status. They're good and I need experts. But no one knows as much about all of our divisions as I do."

That I could believe, if he'd spent his nights and weekends with these books as his friends. No wonder that he'd been successful so fast. What had he done before Hathaway's, then? My father had always referred to Grant as a self-made man, wealthy by his own merits, though I had never cared enough back then to ask how or why.

Grant, it seemed, was a bit of a puzzle. One who was currently looking rumpled, frustrated, manly and very attractive.

"What book would you recommend? For me to start my new well-organized time and mind?"

He rose from the table, tall and contained as he strode to the far end of his shelves. Whatever book he was looking for, he found it immediately.

"Here," he said, stopping a pace away. *The Organized Mind* by Daniel Levitin."

"You actually had this in your office?"

"Yes."

I narrowed my eyes at him. "Did you plant that fortune cookie at the takeout place earlier?"

Grant gave a small, crooked smile. "No. Read it, if you want."

"All right." Our fingers brushed as I took the book from him.

I swallowed. "Thanks. Is it my turn to help you find love in return?"

"I don't need anything in return," he murmured.

"Okay."

The air between us grew quiet and heady. Grant was so close I could feel the faint fragrance of his cologne and his own, masculine scent. When had he become this alluring? Neither of us moved, struck still as if by some enchantment.

"Go home, Ada," Grant said softly. "I'll see you tomorrow."

I nodded, not trusting my voice, gathered up my things and fled.

10

GRANT

Ada put a large stack of manila folders on my desk. "Here are the papers Linda needs you to sign. The ones marked with red contain your briefings for the afternoon meeting and the printed schedule of the conference you're attending next week. Here's a salmon bagel from the place next door. I saw that you didn't have time for lunch today on your schedule."

I had to admit it to myself—she was good. I just didn't have to admit it to *her*.

"With cream cheese?"

"Of course." She gathered up the envelopes in my *to-be-sent* pile and headed out.

"Oh, and Ada?"

"Yes?" She paused just by my door, tossing back her hair to look at me. With her form-fitting dress and impeccable makeup, she looked like a million bucks. If only I could stop noticing that.

"Charles Burch called. He's in town and would like to have dinner with us tonight before the auction tomorrow."

"With the two of us?"

I hated that I liked the way it sounded, *the two of us*, spoken in her voice. This inane infatuation needed to stop.

I nodded to her. "His son is coming along, too. Are you free at eight?"

"Yes." She smiled, as if she looked forward to it. Probably only because Trip was going, I thought darkly. "I'll meet you there. Send me restaurant information?"

"Will do."

The rest of the office cleared out at seven, and I spent the remaining forty-five minutes replying to emails from our international distributors and preparing the week ahead. I had a phone meeting with our office in Japan that, due to the time difference, I could only do now.

I looked myself over in the mirror before heading out, splashed on a bit of extra cologne. An entire evening with a client. I had done it before and would do it again, but that didn't mean I tended to enjoy it. Usually it was meaningless chatter, although Charles had seemed very knowledgeable.

And as stupid as it was, I had to admit to myself that I wasn't looking forward to Trip being there. I knew Ada came from a different world than me, that our upbringings were a thousand miles apart, but I didn't relish the idea of seeing it so clearly.

Although, perhaps that was exactly what I needed. A good, strong shot of reality should cure me of whatever physical attraction I felt for Ada.

I was halfway to the restaurant, walking up Fifth Avenue, when my phone rang. *Ada Hathaway*, the caller ID said. I didn't think she'd ever called me before.

"Yes?"

"I was here early, and they were too, so we went inside. We're having a drink at the bar before they show us to our table. Thought you should know."

My mood soured instantly. She was *early*, so eager was she to meet Trip.

"Good. I'll see you inside."

I didn't wait for her reply, but hung up and quickened my step. The restaurant came into view. *Le Mirage*. French.

"Good evening, Mr. Hathaway." The waiter greeted me. "Your party is inside, having just been shown to the table."

"Thank you." He took my coat and I was led through the darkened interiors to a round table at the back. I saw Ada's blonde hair first, her back to me. She was chatting animatedly—her hands moving as she spoke, and across from her, the two men were watching with sparkling eyes. And how long had this taken? Five minutes? She was like an enchantress.

Charles saw me first. "Mr. Wood, thank you for agreeing to have dinner with us."

"Of course," I replied smoothly. "And call me Grant, if you will."

"I'm Trip," the younger man said, stretching out to shake my hand. He had blue eyes and a pleasant face, the typical American boy look. Perhaps she liked that.

I held his hand in a firm grip. "Grant."

I took the seat they'd left free next to Ada. The sweet scent of perfume hit me, along with the view of skin. She was wearing a silk shift that clung to her frame, enhancing collarbones and fair skin and flushed, rosy cheeks. Thank God I was sitting next to her, and not across, I thought as I picked up the wine list. I would never be able to concentrate on the food.

But then, that meant Trip was opposite her. There really were no good options here tonight.

"The chef has already informed us of the specials," Ada told me. "*Magret du Canard*, which is duck, really quite good. Or the fish of the day—Alaskan halibut."

"Thank you."

Trip leaned forward. "I'd forgotten—you used to study French at school?"

Ada nodded. "But it's many years ago now."

"Still, you were really quite good. That doesn't just go away. Our waiter is French—why don't you test it?"

"Trip," Charles chided. "Ada doesn't have to."

His son gave a playful laugh. "Of course not. But she was the one who actually paid attention in school."

I glanced between them. Paid attention in school, did she?

Ada turned to me with a raised eyebrow as if to say, *What, do you doubt me?*

"By all means," I said. Prove me wrong.

Ada read the challenge in my eyes—I knew she did—and turned back to Trip. "I think I will, then. Go on, gentlemen. Decide what you want and I will do the honors."

One after one we gave our orders to her. Trip made a show of taking what she was having, and I very nearly felt bad for him. Pathetic attempt at flirting if I'd ever seen one.

"*Bonjour, monsieur,*" Ada said to the waiter when he returned. His eyes lit up in anticipation.

"*Bonjour, mademoiselle! Parlez-vous français?*"

"*Un peu.*" Ada laughed. "*Alors, nous voudrions une bouteille d'eau plate et une bouteille de vin blanc, le Sancerre, s'il vous plaît. Je prends le magret de canard et il aura le même. Pour ce monsieur, le poisson du jour. Et pour l'homme à côté de moi*"—here Ada indicated me with a grin to the waiter—"*steak avec des pommes de terre.*"

"*Super,*" the waiter said, scribbling on his notepad. "*Comment le monsieur aimerait-il son steak?*"

"Medium-rare. *Il a des normes très strictes.*" Both the waiter and Ada laughed at that. At my expense, it appeared.

"We'll do our best to accommodate you then, sir," he said to me with a wink and took our menus.

Charles was laughing too, chuckling in his seat.

"You speak French?"

"Enough," he replied, smiling at Ada. "And enough to know that was actually a compliment."

I raised an eyebrow at Ada. Right. She looked back at me with too-earnest eyes. "I just said you had high standards."

The dinner progressed well, after that. The conversation flowed easily around the old man's interest in collecting—he was truly fascinating to speak to. A genuine love for the artifacts, and with a keen interest in what was going to happen with them after the auction.

I assured him we would only part with them in accordance with his own guidelines.

"I look forward to being there," he said. "At the auction."

I hesitated. That wasn't always a good idea. "You're very welcome, naturally. At the same time, I have heard from others that it can be difficult to see the bidding when you have an emotional connection to the items."

He nodded. "I understand them completely. But I think I have to. To make it real."

I glanced over at Ada and Trip. They had been discussing old memories for the past half an hour, Charles seemingly content to let them reminisce. I was not likewise content with this division of conversation.

He saw my sliding focus. "Beautiful, isn't it? With old friends?"

"Yes," I said. "Just beautiful."

Ada saw that we had gone quiet. "We're discussing old teachers," she said. "Not necessarily the most interesting of subjects, but fun nonetheless."

I recognized my moment. The wine had been flowing and the dinner had clearly become more friendly and less professional than I had anticipated. "What was Ada like in school, Trip?"

He gave a wide smile. "Studious, I'd say. Always the belle of the ball, but that hasn't changed, has it?"

"Oh, stop it," she said, but I could see that she looked undeniably pleased.

"They were good kids," Charles said. The fondness in his voice was clear, both for his son and for Ada. Jealousy tore through me, hot and unexpected.

"Yes. Though we didn't have too many classes together, Ada."

"Only math and biology, I think," she mused.

"Yes. I had more classes with Max."

She shrugged, irreverent as always. "I knew there had to be a reason why you were best friends."

Both Trip and Charles laughed, and I smiled too, even as relief rippled through me. So that was why they had a long history together.

Then I took a deep sip of my wine and told myself to quit. She was not mine to feel possessive over—she had never even expressed an interest in me—and that was for the best. We would never work. And I had no interest in wanting to *try* to make it work.

But that was not what my body told me every time she leaned past me to reach for the salt, or the bottle of water, and her bare skin brushed against my arm or her hair swept a fragrant scent past me.

"It's truly awful what happened," Trip said. "I still think about him all the time."

Ada took a sip of her wine, staving off the need to reply for a moment. "So do I."

"What do you do, Trip?" I asked. He blinked, dragging his gaze away from Ada to me. *That's right, asshole,* I thought. *Eyes over here.*

"I work in real estate," he replied. "Mainly in Rhode Island."

The conversation flowed on, and I did my best to engage him and Charles in it. Ada returned to the conversation after a beat, with the same sassy manner as always. But I noticed that she was drinking the wine faster than I was—had she been going at that speed all through the dinner? I hadn't noticed.

Dessert came and went. I settled the bill.

Charles shot us all a grin. "This was a pleasure. I'm looking forward to the auction tomorrow. I trust your judgment implicitly, Grant. Couldn't have found a better custodian."

I was oddly touched by the words. "Glad to hear it."

"We should be heading home, son."

Trip looked over at his dad, and then back at Ada. "Actually, I was wondering if you'd want to go grab a drink after this? Reminisce some more?"

I had to fight the urge to say no, to say we had to work, to do anything at all that would stop them from spending alone time together. It wasn't my place—and it was decidedly not in my interest—but damn if I didn't want to interfere.

And, yet, I'd never heard a sweeter sound than Ada refusing him.

"No thank you, Trip. Grant and I have some things to discuss for work before tomorrow. But it was nice seeing you again, both of you."

They left the restaurant after that—Ada somehow managed to send them on their way, with us staying behind. "Have a nice night now," she told them. "See you tomorrow, Charles."

They'd just disappeared from view—with Trip giving a little glance back like an abandoned puppy—when she downed the rest of her drink and put her head down on the table.

I gazed at her for a moment, blonde hair spilling over smooth arms and linen tablecloth. "So what work thing do you want to discuss?"

She gave a sigh and looked up, only to see that I was smiling. Her frown disappeared. "Thanks for playing along," she said. "I didn't know how to get out of the thing with Trip."

"Don't mention it."

"God, but he can be annoying."

I took a sip of my water to try to hide the grin I felt threatening to spread across my face. "I thought you liked him."

She shook her head slowly, almost lazily, staring at the empty wineglass. "All he wants to do is talk memories and school. Talk talk talk. Incapable of taking a hint, too."

"You're not really friends, then?"

She snorted. "He was one of my brother's idiot buddies

growing up. Only ever interested in the high life. Come, let's go. We've given them enough of a head start."

The retort hovered on my tongue—*isn't that your life too these days?*—but I didn't want her to close off. To my own intense annoyance, I found her fascinating.

"He seemed interested, though." I rose to let her slide out of the seat next to me.

"I was always off-limits as Max's sister. I guess I'm not, anymore." She stumbled slightly on her heels when she stood. I caught her, wrapping my arm around her waist to steady her.

"How much wine did you have?"

"As much as I needed to endure that." She shook her head, bombarding me with her scent again. "Gosh, I'm sorry, Grant."

It was probably the first time I'd heard her speak to me without challenge or menace. "Come. Let's get you home."

"I can walk home, I don't live far from here."

But when I released her she walked slightly unsteadily, so I stepped closer and threaded her arm under mine.

"I'll walk you home. Where to?"

She gave a small, almost helpless chuckle. "Where to?" she repeated. "Grant's taxi firm."

"At your service." I pretended to tip an imaginary hat, and she laughed again. God, but she never had with me before. I could see why fools like Adam and Trip and Sarah wanted to make her laugh again and again and *again.*

"Bon soirée, mademoiselle et monsieur," the waiter told us as we left the restaurant. "Vous faites une tres beau couple."

Ada smiled at him widely. *"Merci,"* she said, but as soon as we left, she broke into laughter.

"What did he say?" I was almost hesitant to ask. I didn't speak French, but I had picked up enough of an under-standing of the Latin languages to be able to make out words and meanings.

"That we make a beautiful couple. Oh, Grant, I didn't have the heart to tell him."

"That we hate each other?"

She laughed again, and I couldn't help but smile. Whatever it was in her that found me amusing tonight made me feel ten feet tall. I needed to get out from under the spell she had me under, and fast.

Ada nodded. "But it was a white lie. I couldn't ruin his night."

"Come along, you drunkard. Where do you live?"

"Fifth and 92nd. I thought you knew."

"How would I know that?"

She shrugged. "You just seem like you'd know."

I didn't quite know how to interpret that comment. Taking her arm again, I set us off at a brisk pace toward her apartment. She walked next to me leisurely, uninhibited and happy in a way that had me guessing she'd be asleep within half an hour.

"Why you'd get into auctioneering?"

"Why do you ask?" And there she went, diving into personal things. She'd practically just admitted to disliking personal discussions, for Christ's sake.

She shrugged. "I'm curious."

"It's a good job. Hathaway's had potential, and I enjoy expanding it."

Ada leaned in closer, so close I could feel the warm exhale of her breath when she spoke. "Lie."

"What?"

"I think you love it. The heat of the auction. The preservation of old artifacts, the chance to see and touch them before they're off to a new owner. The thrill of a new purchase."

"You speak as if *you* love it."

"I'm a Hathaway," she said. "We're given a paddle and a gavel as toys before we can walk."

I snorted. "Right."

We turned a corner. The night air was crisp, a hint of snow in the air, the streets mostly empty.

"You're right, though," I told her after a minute. "I do love it."

"Aha! He finally admits it!"

"Admits what?"

"You do have a heart."

I shook my head at her antics, thrilled nonetheless by the wide smile on her face. Stupid, so stupid, the way I was reduced to a schoolboy around her.

"You're drunk."

"I'm tipsy," she replied. "But I know I'm right. There is something beneath that gravelly exterior."

Gravelly? She was looking more at me than the road ahead—it was a good thing I decided to walk her home. I raised an eyebrow at her. "You make it sound like you've been studying me."

"Perhaps I have." She tried to shrug, but it was hard, her arm still intertwined with mine. "You're interesting."

This was getting dangerous. "I doubt you actually think that."

She stopped dead, turning to me with wide eyes. "Why would you say that? Do you think I'm lying?"

I rolled my eyes and pulled her along. "Not in so many words, no. But you've always made your dislike of me clear."

She was silent for a few moments, probably because this was irrefutable. Ada had practically said it to my face on multiple occasions, and she and her brother had gone out of their way to avoid me at company events before Arthur retired.

"That's not true," she said finally. "I just didn't understand you."

I had to laugh at that. "And you think you do now?"

"Better, at least." Ada shook her head as if to clear it. "You don't make it easy to get to know you."

My mouth settled into a hard line. The words were very

similar to what someone had told me once, many years ago. *You don't make it easy to love you, boy.* And that was in one of the foster homes I'd stayed in longest.

"Come along. We're almost there. Which number are you?" I dragged her forward, perhaps more brusquely than necessary.

"Number seventy-three. Wait." Ada stopped dead again, looking at me with wide eyes. I sighed, exasperated and suddenly very eager to get her inside and go. I felt like running, though it was nearly midnight.

"What now?"

"I didn't insult you now, did I? Oh, I don't want you to close off again." She sighed. "Sometimes I speak first and think after. Actually, that's what I always do."

I shook my head. "Of course not. Come, we're almost at yours."

She took my arm again and walked on in contemplative silence. I could practically feel the thinking going on inside of her head, and half-dreaded, half-anticipated what she'd say next. Uninhibited like this, she seemed like an entirely different person to me. As if she'd forgotten that it was *me* she was talking to, behaving instead like I was one of her good friends.

It scared me that I enjoyed it, being *seen* like that by her.

"You're good at what you do," I told her. "At the firm."

"A compliment, Grant? To little ol' me?" She glanced up at me, momentarily flooring me with the force of her wide smile, entirely devoid of any mockery. "Thank you."

I managed a nod. "Why didn't you do more of it? Before this, I mean."

Ada gave a deep sigh as we stopped outside the entrance of her building. She fumbled to open her purse. I stepped closer and held the straps as she reached inside. I heard the jingle of keys.

A doorman stood outside her building. "Good evening, Miss Hathaway."

She smiled widely at him. "Good evening, Dave. Had a good night?"

"I have. You too, miss?"

Ada nodded at him and reached over to grab my arm again. I hesitated. Technically she didn't need my help anymore. But the gentlemanly thing would be to follow her all the way inside, to her actual front door. It seemed to be what she was expecting.

Logic and emotion warred inside of me. It pained me to watch the former—my constant comrade-in-arms—lose.

We walked through the warm lobby toward the elevators.

"What floor?"

"Twenty-three," she replied, and I pressed it the button. The doors closed and we were alone in the small, confined space. It felt too hot, and too close.

Ada leaned against the dark wood of the elevator and watched me through long lashes. "You asked me why I... why I was just drifting before this internship."

I gave a cautious nod. Drifting was a nice euphemism for what the tabloids and Arthur himself had stated regarding her actions. The girl I had heard of then, spoken about in hushed whispers at charity events and dinners, didn't square up with the healthy-looking one standing before me with resolve in her eyes.

"He died right before my graduation," she said. "Only seven months before. And I fell into my schoolwork as I'd never done before. Yale became the reason I lived and breathed. I think I slept in the library some days because writing essays and memorizing facts was the only way to keep my mind from returning, inevitably, to what I was avoiding."

"But then graduation came," I murmured.

"Yes. And the ground opened up beneath me, and I fell." The elevator door opened and I took her arm—habit now, almost—as she swayed lightly on her feet.

"Number sixteen," she said. "That's me."

I was quiet behind her as she tried to fit her key to the lock. The sudden air between us was heady and comfortable, and I knew that a wrong word from me might break it.

"Whoops." The key slid from her fingers. I bent and took it, finding the keyhole easily.

The door swung open.

She walked inside and I followed, hovering hesitantly by the door. A large living room opened up to floor-to-ceiling windows, the view the same one I had from my apartment.

She tugged off her black coat and slung it over the back of a large, blue sofa. The silver dress she wore clung to every curve. "Thank you for tonight."

"Of course. I'm happy to be your fictional escape from Trip, anytime you need it."

Ada gave a husky laugh, her eyes warm. "You're good at shepherding drunk people."

"I have a lot of practice."

"Have I earned the right to sleep in tomorrow?"

I laughed, despite myself. "Good try. But no."

"Shoot. Well, it was worth a try."

Tomorrow, when all this would be forgotten and she would no longer look at me like that—like I was her friend or confidant.

Like I was one of her favorite people.

"Do you live far away?"

I cleared my throat. "No. In fact, I live right down the street."

"Good. I'd hate to see you have to walk home alone, intoxicated and in the dark."

I smiled. "What would you have done if I did live far away?"

Ada came closer, stopping only a pace away. "I'd have to follow you home," she said seriously. "And then you couldn't leave me there, so you'd follow me home. It would be a never-ending loop, and we'd be caught in a time-space continuum until we eventually died of starvation."

"Death by chivalry."

"Precisely," she declared.

"You're silly."

She shrugged. "You like it."

I did. And I didn't want to leave, despite the fact that I absolutely, most definitely, should. Not only did we have work tomorrow, but she was drunk.

And my intern.

And Arthur's daughter.

And the most interesting person I'd ever met.

"I'll head out. Thanks for tonight."

She nodded, watching me as I began to walk backwards to the elevator. Ada didn't close her front door, not even when I'd pressed the elevator button, our eyes still on one another.

I felt lightheaded, and I didn't think it was the wine.

"Grant?"

I cleared my throat. "Yeah?"

"You know the darkness I was talking about earlier?"

I nodded.

"Well. I'm not falling anymore."

Despite myself, I smiled at her. "I'm glad."

11

ADA

Sleep had always come easily to me as a child. Even as a teenager, I had always slept soundly, from the moment my head hit the pillow until the alarm rang in the morning. After Mom passed, that changed, and after Max, nights became some of the hardest times to make it through.

Which was why—for the longest time—I tried to avoid having to go to bed with my thoughts, to fill the nights with light and laughter and false friends. But tonight there was only silence in my apartment and my bed felt large and empty.

I didn't reach for the image, but it came anyway: Grant in my apartment, hovering awkwardly on the doorstep. I could have invited him in. But the impulse made no sense, and I couldn't have handled his inevitable rejection.

I turned over and snuggled deeper into my pillow, banishing the thought altogether.

But he wouldn't leave. He lingered in my thoughts, a tall, dark figure, his gaze exasperated and increasingly dear. He'd always been handsome, in that aloof, remote way. Only he wasn't remote at all, not when you pressed the right buttons and he came into glorious technicolor.

He was heartbreakingly attractive up close, hands long

and wide. What kind of soft-spoken auctioneer had hands like that? And what might they feel like on my body?

I found that I craved his approval, and that when we spoke, I didn't seek to rile him up anymore. I actually waited for his responses—hung on to his every word. God, what an insipid creature this stupid attraction had made out of me!

I stared up at the ceiling. He would never see me as anything more than a spoiled child. And did I truly want him to? If he looked closer, would he like what he saw? I wasn't sure I did, most days.

Be brave, Ada. Perhaps more like: be foolish.

But I picked up the phone anyway. The impulse was stupid, yes, but persistent. What did I have to lose?

Everything.

Nothing.

So I dialed. The name flickered on my screen around my trembling fingers. *Grant Wood, Hathaway's.* He answered after three eternity-long signals.

"Ada?"

"Hi. Did I wake you?"

"No," he said, but his voice sounded like I had. "Is everything all right?"

"Yes. I just wanted to know what your favorite place in New York is."

There was a loaded silence on the other line. I held my breath, preparing myself for the roar, the outraged *you're calling me at one AM to ask this?*

It didn't come.

"Do you mean Manhattan specifically, or the greater city area?"

"Manhattan," I said. "Unless it makes a big difference for you."

"It doesn't. Am I allowed to be cliché and say the top of the Empire State Building?"

I laughed. "No, you're not."

"The Japanese Reading Room at the Met, then," he said immediately. "That's mine."

"I've never been."

"Most people pass by it. I'm not surprised."

"I should go sometime."

"You should."

I could hear him breathing on the other end, heard the slight sound of him swallowing. I wet my lips, readying myself to speak, but he beat me to it. "Now tell me your favorite place?"

"The statue of Balto in Central Park."

"The dog statue?"

"Yeah. Have you seen it?"

"I've run past it once or twice. But I can't for the life of me think of why it'd be your favorite place?"

"I saw the movie as a kid. He was a hero, you know. Besides, I begged and begged my parents to get us a dog, but we were never allowed to have any pets."

"…so you adopted one in bronze in the park instead."

"See, you're reading my mind."

"Somehow I'm getting used to how it works," he said wryly.

"I wasn't really trying to call you, you know. Your number is actually just one off from Fratelli's pizza just down the street from me."

Grant's low chuckle reached me across the line, sent shivers down my spine. "Lucky me."

"And who knows? I might misdial again," I murmured.

There was a long silence. "You probably shouldn't," he finally said. "But I hope you do."

———

Work continued as usual, with no hint that anything had happened during that evening or late at night. Our phone calls remained secret, even to our waking selves, it seemed.

A week passed, until I found myself all dressed up and at yet *another* company event. We had plenty of those—but at least I was getting the full use out of my formal wear.

I took a sip of my glass of champagne. Grant was silent beside me as he looked out over the milling guests. He had been quiet, speaking little and only when necessary to the various division heads, guests and staff that approached him. As much as his reputation preceded him, so did his aloofness; I knew several of the division heads were just as baffled by him now, seven years later, as they had been when Dad first brought him on.

His profile was stark and handsome, and he struck me suddenly as a painting, distant and imposing and deceptively flat. I wanted to break him out of it. I wanted him to come alive.

A thought struck me, silly and wonderful at the same time.

"Hey, have you ever been to the basement levels? Minus four?"

Grant turned to me, brows furrowed. "The storage vaults? Yes. Infrequently."

"Aren't they the best?"

He shook his head with an amused smile, and just like that, he became a person again, human and present. "You never cease to surprise me, Ada. And what did you do down there? Hide from your responsibilities?"

"Very funny." I made sure the bartender wasn't looking and reached behind the open bar. My hand found the neck of a champagne bottle easily. "And that's exactly what we're going to do."

His eyes widened as I snuck it out and under my arm. "Ada—"

"If you've never been to storage when it's empty, you haven't lived."

Grant raised a dubious eyebrow at that. I decided he

needed a bit more convincing, and pressed the button to the nearby elevator.

"Come on, you're supposed to be the CEO of this place? Doesn't that mean you have to know its ins and outs? No one's looking." I jerked my chin toward the throngs of people. "And you've already spoken to everyone."

He watched me for a long second, eyes hazel and steady, his hands in his pant pockets. I thought he looked amused—I had been trying to rile him up, after all—but it might've just been my imagination.

The elevator gave a loud ding.

"Last chance to escape," I said, waving the bottle of Taittinger enticingly, and stepped into the elevator. My breath came fast with adrenaline and nerves and the joy that always came from a bout of verbal sparring with him.

He didn't follow. I sighed, watching the doors close.

A hand reached between them as they were inches from snapping shut. With a groan of protest they opened again.

"I couldn't very well let you finish an entire vintage bottle by yourself," Grant said and hit the button for -4.

I hid a smile against my shoulder. Perhaps he enjoyed our little games as much as me, after all.

The hallway was deserted and required several bouts of security clearance to access. Grant's hands were sure and able on the various panels, typing eight and twelve-digit codes and using his fingerprints for the final section. I wondered what they'd feel like tracing my lips, and then flushed at the thought.

The lights of the storage room flickered on. It was vast, all wide shelves and boxes and carefully planned layouts. A kingdom to be explored, a treasure trove of things to be sold and bought.

"Why did you come down here, anyway?"

"I was here often as a kid," I told him, leading the way through the carefully placed boxes and rows. They were filled with items scheduled for auction, values already estimated and photos taken. There was a good reason for all the security measures—the thick concrete walls and the extreme fire safety precautions. Millions of dollars' worth of items sat in these rooms.

But the best things were in the back.

"Come," I told him, finding the gray iron door. It wasn't locked and opened easily.

"The tomb?" Grant asked skeptically, ducking under the low door to enter the vault. It was a massive storage space. Boxes and crates stood in disarray, with blankets tossed over. Some were dusty and gray with disuse, others looked like they'd been put there only last month. Everything that Hathaway's couldn't sell went here. From estate sales, failed auctions... The tomb housed it all.

"All of this is useless."

"It is *absolutely not* useless. And that's coming from me, arguably the most useless of them all."

He snorted. "I didn't mean that, you know."

"I know," I said dismissively, though I hadn't. His assurance did weird things to my chest. "Oh look, it's still here! Come have a seat."

Somewhat reluctantly, Grant sat down on the dusty brocade sofa at the end of the aisle. It had been there since I was a toddler, a relic of good memories and nostalgia.

Grant looked like a model for a high-fashion magazine or an eccentric photography shoot, dressed in an expensive, tailored suit but seated in a dimly lit vaulted storage space. Beside him was a wonky lamp, and the couch he reclined on was probably from the 18th century.

Grant reached up and ran a hand through his thick hair, only increasing the beautiful way his rugged looks melded with the surroundings.

"What are you looking at?"

"You." I pretended to capture a photograph of him. I could see the headlines; A portrait of the enigmatic CEO of Hathaway's, youngest in the company's history.

Grant flushed slightly and looked away. "So why did you come here as a kid? Is this the Hathaway child-rearing version of the naughty corner?"

I unwrapped the champagne paper and carefully twisted the metal cage open.

"No. It was more like a paradise. Sometimes, when we were kids, we'd come here and explore, especially when Dad was busy upstairs or we were waiting to be picked up by my mother."

The cork came undone with a small satisfying *pop*. I took a sip straight from the bottle only to find Grant watching me. I passed it to him and he accepted, following suit. There was something strangely intimate about sharing a drink together like that—mouth to mouth, as it were. I'd rarely seen it that way before, but suddenly I could think of nothing else than the fact that Grant's lips had just touched the same place mine were.

"You were really allowed to roam around down here, unsupervised?" Grant shook his head. "Thanks for informing me. I'll have to strengthen security in the future."

I laughed. "It's all about having an in, you see. One of the security guards was amazing—Hank. He used to show me and Max around when we had nothing to do but wait. He'd take us back here to this vault, and he'd make up stories about these items."

Grant took another sip from the champagne bottle and loosened the tie at his neck. "Make up stories?"

"Yes. 'This might look like a boring blue-and-white vase. But no! It once housed the ashes of the great emperor of China thousands of years ago before it was smuggled to New York through a secret chain of international pirates, all fighting to get this vase.'"

"That's a terrible story." Grant laughed.

"I'm improvising over here."

"What a legend though."

"Me? Why, thank you."

"Hank."

"I wonder if he still works here." I frowned. "He won't get in trouble because I told you this, will he? If so, it was a pseudonym. His actual name isn't Hank."

"Nice save." Grant's eyes sparkled, and I felt like the champagne, all bubbly inside. Those memories had only lived between me and Max, and now one more person knew. Perhaps that was what people meant when they spoke about enjoying a loved one's memory. It was about sharing it.

"Thank you."

"No, he won't be punished. How could I? He should get a raise, being forced to drag around two little bratty children like that."

"Hey!" Grant ducked hastily at the old fan I aimed at his head. It hit the back of the sofa harmlessly. He was laughing so hard he had to put the bottle down on the floor.

"These are precious artifacts, Ada. Look, but don't touch," he breathed between chuckles.

"And these are not to be gotten rid of, by the way, in case your organizing mind has already begun walking down that route. I didn't show you this just so you could trash it."

He handed me the bottle and stood, walking over beside me to look over the motley assortment of goods Hathaway's had kept for decades. "I did know that this existed before, you know."

"Yes, but knowing and seeing are two different things."

"Quite true. Like, I knew Ben Harris was an arrogant asshole, but I didn't see it until he became Jack and Thorn's CEO."

I shook my head at him and raised a finger. "No, now you're thinking. The whole point of this was to drink champagne and get you *out* of your statue-like, brooding mood. I won't have it, not in my storage room, no sir."

Grant laughed again. It struck me that he had done that a lot tonight, and that the sound echoed tantalizingly against this wide room, dark and rich. He wasn't a man to indulge in wine or spirits, but he'd likely had a glass more than usual. Maybe that did him good.

"Tell me. What's your favorite piece in this room?"

"My favorite piece?"

"Yes. If you've been here so often, I mean." Grant leaned back against a stack of boxes, looking stupidly handsome and heady. It wasn't that he became less imposing with time, I thought, only that you somehow got used to it. It inspired you to rise to his level.

And at the moment, his eyes glittered with challenge.

I found a small oil lamp, perfect in shape and color, tucked away behind a stack of chairs.

"Aha!" I said, turning around dramatically. "Behold, the—"

"No," Grant interrupted. "Too cliché."

I frowned. "But *Aladdin* is a classic."

"No bidders on that. Sorry." Grant shrugged. "I don't make the rules."

I rolled my eyes at him but continued, passing by an old oriental rug. That was out, too, then, I assumed.

After nearly three minutes of perusal I found a portrait of a young, curly-haired man. I held it up gingerly. The frame felt fragile in my hands.

"The youth here was consumed by his own vanity," I said sadly. "Trapped forever inside this portrait, forced to live a lonely existence, doomed never to be able to see himself again."

"*The Picture of Dorian Gray*," Grant observed. "Oscar Wilde. You're getting better, but I have a feeling Hank was more creative than this, Ada. No more plagiarism."

"You're impossible."

"So I've been told."

The room had countless dusty treasures. What would satisfy him? A thought struck me, and I grinned. "Well, well, well. What have we found here?" I stalked back to where he sat. "The item sitting here is the most unique of them all. The

CEO of Hathaway's in the flesh. But whatever is he doing inside the tomb? That, kids, is one magical tale."

Grant raised an eyebrow. "Careful now."

"He didn't heed the advice of the magical fortune cookie delivered to him by a very kind, very beautiful fairy-intern."

"You?"

I shushed him. "Don't interrupt the storyteller. It's rude. Anyway, he just continued on with his successful existence. You see, this was not an ordinary man. No, the CEO of Hathaway's was the best in all regards, except in his ability to smile. He did it very rarely."

Grant's small grin was proving something quite to the opposite, but I ignored it and carried on. "He didn't heed the advice. He didn't seek love. He didn't learn how to smile. And so he eventually became obsolete, forced to stay here in the tomb, because of a lack of bidders."

"The poor CEO who never got sold," Grant said. "That makes for a beautiful title of a children's book."

"It would be an instant bestseller." I reached for the bottle.

"With a movie adaption in the immediate works."

"You'd be played by Brad Pitt."

"Isn't he what, twenty-five years older than me?"

"But still Brad Pitt." I shrugged. "Sorry."

"You're nothing like your father, you know?"

I jumped up on one of the large wooden crates, letting my legs dangle. "Yes. And doesn't he know it."

"You've been an asset since you joined, you know."

I shook my head at him. "You're thinking again."

Grant came closer, stopping a pace away. He reached for the champagne bottle but didn't take it, our hands touching against the cool glass.

"I can't stop it," he said softly. "It's what I do."

"Then analyze my story a little deeper," I said. My heart was beating fast, faster than the situation warranted. But I'd never had all of his attention like this—and all the attention of a man like Grant Wood was a lot for one woman to handle.

The side of his mouth curved up slightly as his gaze burned into mine. Wherever it touched, I burned; my cheeks, my nose, my lips. I felt just as hungry. I watched the rise of his cheekbones and the hazel of his eyes as if trying to memorize him. I'd never been able to study him this close before.

"Look," he said. "I'm smiling."

I gave a small, breathy laugh. "Wow. Alert the media."

He tugged the bottle from my hand and put it aside without our gaze breaking. My knees brushed against his thighs as he came closer, naturally spreading to allow him space. The wool of his suit was soft against the silk and skin.

He seemed to hover on the precipice, wanting and willing and undecided. His eyes flicked back to my lips. God, but I didn't think I had ever anticipated a kiss this much.

"I'm not a precious artifact," I whispered. "You can both look and touch."

I heard the ragged intake of his breath. Grant's hands found my waist, holding me like I was the Ming vase from the story before. Precious and ancient and magical.

And then he touched his lips to mine. He kissed me like it was all he'd ever wanted, ever needed, as if I was water and he was dying of thirst, and I knew that this was all I'd ever wanted too.

I could feel the fight within him, as if he was restraining himself still, so I clawed at his dinner jacket and tugged at the hair at the nape of his neck. It was as soft as I'd imagined, and he groaned into my mouth.

I wanted him to let go, to lose himself in me like I was losing myself in him. And he did. Grant's tongue met mine, demanding and hesitant all at once. I'd never been kissed like this before and I pushed him away just enough to tell him so decisively.

"Off," I said. He smiled and tugged off his dinner jacket in one quick move, returning to my arms the next. My legs wrapped around his waist of their own volition, and I twined myself around him like a vine to a tree, arms around necks and hands inside shirts.

Grant kissed my cheek, my throat, desire coursing up my body like flames with his every touch. I pulled his shirt up from his pants, eager to find the hot skin of his abdomen, of his back, seeking anything that might fuse us closer together.

His hands traced the back of my thighs and I inched closer, eager for any friction. "So beautiful," he murmured against my lips.

We kissed as the silk fabric of my dress slowly rose higher, encouraged by both of our movements.

There was no thinking, no planning, only this; instinct and heat. His hands brushed up over my inner thighs and I sighed into his mouth. Higher they reached, smoothing over soft skin until one knuckle stroked against my clit.

Grant smiled against my mouth at the reaction he elicited, touching me masterfully through the thin lace of my underwear.

His tongue traced my bottom lip and I moaned, twisted my hands in his hair, and let all my desire and frustration pour into his kisses. Grant slid my panties to the side and then he was touching me, parting folds, stroking and playing and I knew I was going to die here of desire, of want. No woman could handle being the object of his intense focus and determination.

"Beautiful," he repeated, and then his lips left mine. I growled in frustration only to see him drop softly to his knees and flick my silken dress up entirely, so that I was bared to his gaze.

"Grant?"

"Ada," he murmured and bent his head between my legs. I couldn't help the moans of pleasure that echoed through the storage room. Grant's tongue was precise and effective, loving me like I was all he'd ever wanted to taste.

It had never been like this before.

"No one can hear you but me," he said, and I felt the

warm breath of his voice against sensitive skin. "I want to hear you scream."

And I did. His hands and mouth wouldn't allow for any other reaction, as I lay splayed out before him on a crate with my arm thrown over my face. I'd never felt so vulnerable but also so perfectly desired. Entirely wanted.

My orgasm built steadily, vaulted and crested until I shattered under his hands, broke apart in that empty vault. An instrument played expertly by his skill—a master at work.

"God," I murmured, fingers idly sliding through his hair. "*God.* What was *that?*"

He gently slid my underwear back into place, the soft movement brushing against sensitive flesh. I winced. Grant grinned as he rose before me. Soft hands smoothed my silken skirt back down over my legs.

I grasped his shoulders and pulled him to me. The fire in me was temporarily sated, but being close to him was more than enough to make me burn again.

"Ada," he murmured against my clavicle. My hands were hunting, searching for him, for the buckle of his belt. He felt so hard against my hand that it must be painful and my insides clenched at the idea of having him within me.

Grant caught my wrists and I could hear him swallow. "No," he said. "We can't. Not here."

The refusal seemed almost comical. What we'd just done... that was acceptable here? I nipped at his lower lip. "Why?"

"I didn't exactly bring protection with me," he said, leaning his head against my shoulder again.

"Oh." Of course. And while it seemed I could make Grant lose control for a while, I probably couldn't all the time. "Poor little CEO indeed."

He laughed silently against my skin, and slowly, both of our breaths returned to normal.

He straightened with a sigh. "Come, angel. They'll be looking for us." Grant lifted me up and down from the crate.

My gray dress fell in a waterfall around my legs, hiding all evidence of our liaison. The endearment fell easily from his lips and I couldn't help but smile.

"That was probably the best story ever told down here," I told him. My cheeks felt flushed, too heated, and I couldn't quite look at him but I couldn't really look away, either.

Grant gave me a crooked smile as I reached up to pat his mussed hair down. He bent to give me better access and I smoothed it back, till it was presentable once more.

"My bad," I murmured.

"It's one of the risks you take." He shrugged slightly before grabbing the bottle of champagne and my hand.

The elevator ride up was one of action and nerves. I fixed my hair and tried to pat some of the frantic, flushed heat from my cheeks away with the cool champagne bottle.

Grant tucked his shirt back into his pants and turned once more into the tall, imposing man beside me, his face indecipherable.

"And so the show goes on," I murmured, pulling at the hem of my dress.

Grant kissed the back of my hand with featherlight lips just as the elevator slid to a smooth halt. "It always does."

12

GRANT

Damn.

Everything had been going just great. We'd found a wary middle ground, one where she didn't push me too far and I'd manage to mostly forget that she was interning here. And then she had gone and flashed me that large, brilliant smile and flicked her hair and asked if *I wanted to see something cool* and I'd followed her like an overgrown puppy.

If only it hadn't been for that dress. The way the silk had wrapped around her slender form, reflecting shimmery in the low light. And the sheer nerve, of grabbing a bottle from behind the bar.

Like she hadn't given a damn. Like she had as little interest in the people there as I did.

Like I was the only one she was interested in talking to.

This was spinning out of control, and it was doing so *fast*. I couldn't have an employee—an intern—that I didn't know how to handle in the office. And I damn well couldn't complicate things with Arthur's daughter, his only remaining child. The man deserved better than to have her happiness tarnished. And I would tarnish it eventually, one way or another, if we continued down this path.

Women never stayed with me and I never invited them to

do so. It was always transactional in nature, a polite dance that ended in mutual satisfaction and eventual polite disengagement. Well-bred, interesting women who enjoyed my company and the things my money could buy. Not one had made jokes about me the way Ada had.

The poor CEO who didn't get sold.

This would only end one way if I didn't find some way to temper both of our expectations right now.

It was easy to spot her, a golden and gray flame at the far end of the room Hathaway's had rented for the event. Her head was thrust back in a laugh, talking to two of the division heads for the company. As if she hadn't just had my head between her thighs. As if I hadn't just given her the best goddamn orgasm of her life.

As if I hadn't had the best sexual encounter of *my* life.

Desire and frustration coursed through me, darkening my voice and countenance. We needed to talk, and not here. Not with all these people. Did she really enjoy those two fools anyway?

I shook my head to clear it and reached for another glass of champagne. I'd hired both of them myself; they were great experts in their respective fields. I refused to be jealous of them.

So I found a table next to them instead, watching her in my peripheral. A moment would come when I might be able to set us straight. Make things clear… or clearer, at least.

"Mr. Wood. A splendid occasion."

I glanced down at Marc in surprise. I hadn't known he would be here. He'd been Arthur's hire, but the man was worth his weight in gold.

"Yes," I agreed.

"Might I pick your mind about something?"

"Of course," I said. *If you must.*

"Have you heard about Jack and Thorn's new CEO?"

"Naturally. They changed leadership just a week ago."

"He's young."

I glanced sideways to Ada; a few of the other interns from other divisions had joined her. Both young women and men crowded around her, eager to share in some of the star power. I saw looks of both admiration and envy. Of course; they'd gained their positions through our regular recruitment system.

"He is. But he's been working in the company for many years," I said. "We'll have to keep an eye out for Jack and Thorn's potential changes in operating practices, of course."

"Yes. I'll make sure that we pay a careful eye to how their marketing evolves under his leadership."

"Good." If Ben Harris was going to try to steal our significant market share—I had no doubt that was his aim—he'd have to wrest it from my cold, dead hands. Hathaway's would not fade under my control.

Snippets from nearby conversation drifted over to us. As a post-graduate degree is a requirement for most departments, it'd be fun to hear what you studied for your masters? I heard a nasal voice say, and then Ada's smooth response; I have an undergraduate degree in art history from Yale.

"If you'll excuse me," I said to Marc. "We'll continue this conversation in the office."

The interns fell quiet as I approached; the divisions selected them in combination with HR, and while I recognized most of them I'd only ever spoken with one or two. Ada looked up at me, her blue eyes guarded.

"Ladies and gentlemen. I hope you're enjoying the festivities."

"We are, Mr. Wood," a gangly boy said. "Thank you very much."

"I'm not the one to thank. It is company policy that all employees, including interns, attend company events. I'm glad to see you all here. Ada, I need your input for the Smith auction on Monday."

"Of course." She grabbed her purse and hurried to my side in a flurry of gray silk. For an insane moment, I felt the urge to reach for her hand, to see what it would be like if we attended these things together. If we went everywhere as an *us*. I choked down the absurd impulse.

We weaved through the crowd silently, knowing that we had the eyes of the interns on us.

"Do you often get that?"

She sighed. "So you heard?"

"Only parts."

Ada was silent as we approached the terrace. "Sometimes. It's only natural, I suppose, and it doesn't bother me."

It bothered me. It was true that I had resented her intrusion into the executive branch, the unconventional way she'd been shoe-horned into this, but there was no denying that she was doing an excellent job. Not even I could be so much of an ass as to not notice.

"If anything gets worse, you come to me," I said and leaned over the railing. The New York air was cold and I could see goose bumps on her bare arms. She didn't complain. I swallowed against the impulse to give her my suit jacket. I was here to set things straight—not to act the gentleman. It would not be fair to encourage her to think that way of me.

"All right." She leaned back against the railing and looked at me with a cocked eyebrow. "Did you really bring me out here to talk about the Smith auction? Or to finish what we started?"

Damn her for being so incredibly alluring. The iron railing was smooth and worn under my painfully tight grip. "To talk. But not about auctions."

"Good. I don't think I could handle a business lecture now."

"I wanted to apologize for earlier."

Her look of blunt surprise made the whole thing about ten times better—I'd have done it for that look alone. "You're apologizing to me?"

"Yes," I said calmly. "You are my intern. It was unprofessional."

She leaned against the railing with a crooked smile. The light pink of her lipstick was far less noticeable now; knowing that I was the one who had kissed it off made standing this close to her an exercise in willpower.

"Entirely," she offered. "But I don't think either of us truly minded."

I snorted. "Perhaps not. The physical aspect is clearly… there. But it's not something we can indulge in."

"Wow. Not even an hour later, and you're already coming with the 'don't get too attached' spiel. Are you this charming to the women you actually date?"

I slid my gaze to hers in frustration. Mirth played across her features, and she was clearly mocking me. Very well then. I could play along.

"No, I normally just flash my credit card. You're getting the VIP treatment."

She laughed, the sound like a pattering of rain and sunshine, and not for the first time I thought of how much easier my life would have been if her father hadn't engineered her internship.

"What a catch you are, Grant."

I snorted—I certainly wasn't. I should be happy that she had realized that. "What happened can't happen again, Ada."

"Despite us both being mature, consenting adults about it?" Her hand trailed the iron railing, stopping perilously close to mine.

"Despite that. It won't lead anywhere, it's unprofessional, and it's beneath both of us to engage in such behavior. Come on. You don't even like me."

She gave a thoughtful nod. "That's true. We've never been friends. My final offer, sir—I'll honor your terms if you honor mine. We try being friends."

She reached out her hand to me, slender and soft, with

long fingers that had only an hour ago been threaded through my hair. On my chest. Inching their way downwards.

I gave a gruff nod. "Fine," I said and shook her hand.

Friends.

We were playing with fire, and we both knew it.

13

ADA

Grant's refusal made perfect sense. In fact, there was nothing between us anyway apart from an interest in the well-being of the company and the internship. He'd always made it clear that success and Hathaway's came first, not to mention the fact that I'd never seen him in any long-term relationships.

Besides, I knew I was a mess. And I couldn't be with someone who would inevitably leave me. There was only so much pain a person could handle, and somehow, I knew that my share was full.

And yet, for thirty minutes, the world had narrowed. It had just been us two in that storage room, Grant and Ada, no last names or positions or jockeying. Only heat and lust and a desire to fuse—a desire that refused to leave me.

I was explaining all of this to Minna, who was sprawled on her back in my living room with a heavy book across her chest.

"It doesn't matter anyway," she said. "Your couple name would either have been Grada or Ant, and both suck."

I burst out laughing. Trust unique, crazy Minna to give me the real truth.

"And you've regularly told me how hard he's been on you since you started working there, not to mention that he's your father's busboy. Don't you want to get out from under his thumb?"

Everything she was saying was *technically* correct, based on the information I'd given her.

"Well…"

"What? Ada, don't tell me you're starting to like him?"

I sighed. "Maybe. Look, it's not like *that*, okay. It's more of an… infatuation. A stupid attraction. Nobody can drive me as crazy as him." And nobody, *nobody*, kissed like him. With single-minded determination and sensual focus.

"There's more, too. I can see that the strong exterior he puts up is a facade, and if I could only get him to drop it for a moment…"

"You have a savior complex," Minna declared. "I'm sure I've read about this somewhere, perhaps Freud… or Jung…"

"No, no, I don't want you to diagnose this. Just tell me what to do."

"What to do about Grant?"

"Yes."

"You, Ada Hathaway, are asking me for advice with men?"

"Yes." It was true that my experiences with men the last two years had been far and few between, and often disasters from start to finish. And they'd never been anyone I'd cared remotely enough to talk to my girlfriends about.

Minna sat up straight and put her hand on her heart. I rolled my eyes at her supercilious manner.

"Okay, so this is my advice."

"Yes," I said impatiently. "Lay it on me."

"Continue doing a kick-ass job. Show him that this doesn't become you—so what if he doesn't want to be physical again? Doesn't mean you can't be friends or have a cordial relationship. If he wants to get all weird about it, let him. He's right about one thing—he is still your boss for the next month and a half. So don't screw it up."

My eyes widened. "Minna. That was actually good advice."

"I've been known to bestow it from time to time."

"But, does it get me closer to what I want?"

"And what do you want?"

To kiss Grant. To feel his lips on my skin again, to shed his layers and feel his body against mine. "Him," I said simply. "It's not a good idea in any shape or form, but I want *him.*"

She gave me a crooked smile. "Hey, that's why you play along for now. Don't let him write you off as a child or a spoiled intern. Prove to you both that you're mature."

I reached over and flicked her nose, a gesture Max had always done to me. "What would I do without you?"

———

Conveniently enough, Grant and Adam left for a three-day work trip the following day. "I'll be available by phone," he told the office before they left. "Keep me informed about the Old Masters auction and the new marketing campaign, and ensure that the advertising for the upcoming Charity Auction goes as planned."

We'd all nodded and agreed and said our *yes sirs,* and then he'd ducked out of the office as if he hadn't just left a young woman he'd recently had a very intense and intimate moment with.

I had given him a cool wave and then turned my back, returning to my work on the computer. Two could play that game, mister.

Hell, I'd practically invented it.

I needed this internship to get my trust fund. And I enjoyed it far too much to jeopardize anything, especially for someone who'd just made it very clear that he was not interested in anything beyond the physical sense. Not that I was either, I reminded myself. Getting the heart involved would inevitably complicate things, and there was no way I was going to risk getting hurt.

I sent a quick text to Minna after lunch with a sunglass emoji.

Ada: If I played it any cooler I'd be frozen solid.

Minna: Damn, ice queen. Make him cold enough to long for your warmth.

Ada: Wow. You could probably write smut, you know?

Minna: Please. As if I don't already.

I laughed and returned to the task at hand, designing the layout and marketing plan for the upcoming Charity Auction. Hathaway's hosted it every year, and the ball was practically the highlight of our events calendar.

The days passed quicker than I had anticipated without Grant to anchor my days around. Hathaway's was a crossroads of a place, goods coming and going daily and everything managed by the executive section. Every day, it seemed, I learned more about the business side of art, about things I'd never thought of before.

"I have to rush for lunch with my sister," Linda said as we bumped into one another by the elevators. "These just came for Mr. Wood. Would you mind just putting them on his desk?"

"Of course." I took the files from her, curious at the light weight. The folder was entirely blank—not marked by any name or logo.

Grant's office felt large without his presence in it, the books dusty and neglected despite it only having been three days since they'd last been seen by their owner. They must feel his absence keenly.

I knew I did.

He'd left his desk in fastidious order. Not a pen or a folder was out of place. No personal effects, either. Not a portrait of his family or an old diploma.

I dropped the files on his desk, but as I did so, something

slid out and fluttered to the floor. A photograph, slightly yellowed around the edges.

It felt stiff in my fingers. A young boy looked up at me, hazel eyes narrowed in suspicion. Thick, unruly hair hung down past his forehead and curled around his ears. There was a large farm in the background with a rusty truck. Despite the clear sky and the sunshine, the freckled boy did not look happy. He was also very thin, hunched around the shoulders as if he'd already learned that turning inwards was the best solution to the hardships of the world.

I flipped it over. Someone had scribbled a name and date in black, sharp letters. *Graham Woodhouse, age eleven, fostered by the Eltons.*

With shaking hands, I opened the file only to see the listed name of the New York Social Services Records at the top. I put the picture carefully back inside and shut the file, backing away from the desk as if he was there to see me. Maybe he was—he didn't strike me as a man to put cameras in his office, but you never knew.

You never knew. Grant Wood, also known as Graham Woodhouse. Foster homes. *No family,* he'd said. No university. Everything I knew about him rearranged around this new information.

Reticence with sharing personal details, a desire for order and rules. The sudden appearance at my father's side at the age of twenty-four, already a self-made millionaire several times over.

Was he digging into his past? Why had he searched for this? Curiosity dug its claws in me and all the answers might just be in that file, right at my fingertips.

But he'd not only hate me for it when he found out, but I knew he'd retreat from it. I couldn't do that to Grant. So I filed the information away and carefully closed the door to his office.

I didn't admit it to Minna—and hardly even to myself— but I googled Graham Woodhouse that evening and read through nearly eight pages of results. But I saw nothing that seemed to relate to the Grant I knew.

I could hardly sleep on Thursday night, knowing that he'd be in the office on Friday, back from the trip. At eight AM sharp he'd give a rundown of what he and Adam had accomplished, standing before us in his well-tailored suit.

Minna came over with sushi and decided we needed to choose an outfit that would make him regret his decision. She seemed to be a lot more willing to hang out since I started my internship, and I knew it had to do with the simple fact that I wasn't partying or spending time with my old party friends anymore, one Vivienne Hurst in particular.

When one faded, the other one came back. I found that I preferred Minna's company anyway.

"Choose the navy blue dress. He'll go crazy for it," Minna said.

I supposed he might. It was the type of sleek, professional attire that most at Hathaway's dressed in, and almost a female version of the sleek suits Grant wore. I looked at myself in the mirror, at the blonde hair swept back and the professionally clean look. Two years ago, I would never have thought I'd be excitedly planning outfits for work at my father's firm.

For *Grant Wood.* Or Graham Woodhouse, whatever he liked to call himself. The image of him as a child came back to mind, distrustful eyes staring into the camera and messy too-long hair. *The poor CEO who never smiled.* Perhaps it wasn't that off-mark after all.

"Good morning, Ada." Linda's smile was all sunshine the next day. "You look great today."

"Thanks."

"Going somewhere tonight?"

"Yes, please tell us about any hot date plans you have," Sarah said as she made her way to the conference room, files ready for the morning meeting. "I'm starved for adult discussion."

"The kids driving you wild?" I smiled at her. Sarah had

two small daughters who kept her up in the evenings, watching *Frozen* on repeat and raiding her makeup kit.

"Yes," she said with a sigh. "Now tell us. Any plans?"

"None." I laughed. "And I'm not dating anyone right now. Where is everyone? We're set to start soon."

Adam came into the room with a huff, dropping his brief-case in the corner and pushing his slightly askew glasses back in place. "Sorry I'm late!"

"You're not. You have ten minutes to spare," Sarah said patiently.

He glanced at his watch. "Oh. Right. Well, we might as well start now—everyone's here."

"Grant's not," I pointed out. "He's always the one to start us off."

"He's not coming today." Adam busied himself with passing around the day's briefing documents, just as well-formatted and prepared as usual. He finally looked up to see all three of us staring at him.

"And why not?" Linda asked. "There's nothing in the schedule about him being out of office."

"Mr. Wood called me on my way in. He's sick. Caught something in Seattle, I think," Adam said.

He was sick. *He was sick.*

"So he's taking a day off?" Sarah blinked, her papers forgotten in hand. "He's never done that before."

"Someday has to be the first, I guess." Adam shrugged and took a seat at the head of the table, clearly eager to get on with the day.

I followed suit, looking at the briefing in my hand but not seeing it. He had to be doing this to avoid me. But the suspicion didn't feel right, either, because that would mean he was either a coward or neglectful in his work, and I'd certainly never seen him do the latter.

"Did he sound sick? When he called you?"

Adam looked up at me with confusion and slight irritation on his features. I'd interrupted his introductory rundown of the past day's events and blushed. It was stupid to be this inexplicably interested in Grant's whereabouts, and yet I couldn't stop myself.

"Yes," Adam replied. "Now, it's imperative that we help the divisions with whatever they need before the weekend. The expert on forgeries we used to employ for the Old Masters and British Paintings has quit, unfortunately, and is relocating. We'll need to call in someone else. Sarah, can you handle that?"

She nodded.

The day continued.

But the nagging suspicion didn't leave. Grant and I might have been approaching some form of tentative friendship last week, but now we were practically strangers—strangers intent on avoiding one another.

I spent the evening reorganizing my closet—a sure sign that something was amiss, as I never did it when happy or at peace. I went to brunch the following Saturday with old high school friends, the type you know well enough to complain to but not quite enough to be honestly happy for their successes. They showed off photos of travels and engagement rings and new apartments, each seemingly trying to one-up the other.

Yeah, that wasn't happening again any time soon. I'd settled for relationships that gave me nothing for far too long —likely before Max had died too. Perhaps it was time that I re-arranged my personal life as well, cut out people like shallow high school friends and party people, and spend more time with old friends like Minna and new friends like Sarah.

Fifth and 93rd, Grant had said once. Which meant he did indeed live up the street from me.

And if he had been avoiding me by not coming to work the day earlier, there was one very quick way of remedying that. I had exactly one month left of this internship, and things would get awkward real fast if this wasn't resolved.

But just in case he actually was sick... I'd need an excuse. An excellent, foolproof plan formed in my mind.

Putting on re-reruns of *The Office*, I hunted through my kitchen cabinets for the old, stained recipe book my mom had once cherished. I'd snuck it from the kitchen of our family apartment for my second year of college, hoping neither Max nor Dad would notice. Neither did.

The smell of homemade chocolate macadamia cookies spread through my kitchen forty minutes later. I packed them up in a small glass Tupperware box, stuffed myself into my warmest, wooliest coat and headed down the street.

His name was listed as *Wood* inside with the concierge, on floor 32. I gave the receptionist my best smile, fluttering my eyelashes a little, and held up my freshly baked cookies.

"Grant's sick," I said. "I want to surprise him. Would you mind sending me up to his floor?"

The old man behind the desk sniffed. "Smells fantastic. Of course. I can't imagine Mr. Wood would be sad to see you."

I returned his smile and made my way to the elevators, puzzling over that comment. Was it a compliment to me? Or because he regularly brought so many women up to his apartment that it was basically commonplace for the recep-tionists to just let them into the building?

Shaking my head, I focused on what I was going to say. Nerves fluttered through my stomach. This had seemed like such a foolproof, fun plan at home. Surrounded by the steel and glass of this strange, new elevator on my way to his apartment, it felt silly. More evident of the foolish girl he thought I was than the mature woman I was sure he wanted. The fear of being dismissed gnawed in me.

His was the only door in the corridor that opened before me. *Wood*. Not even *Grant* was listed, as if the ability to be imposing and anonymous was so important to him that it extended even to his front door.

I swallowed. *Don't be a coward, Ada.* I had been for far too long, anyway, hiding from life and from feeling.

I pressed the doorbell.

The long, agonizing wait that followed felt like an eternity. The door finally swung open.

"Ada?" Grant was dressed in a pair of dark blue slacks and a gray T-shirt, arms bare. His thick hair was not combed back or styled, but curled adorably at his temples. There was an intimacy in his homeliness, the dressed-down version of the normally button-upped CEO, and I felt myself blush. I couldn't remember the last time I had—and it had certainly not been for a man fully dressed, just because he happened to be in his casual wear.

"What are you doing here?" He asked, seeing as I hadn't responded. My mouth felt dry.

"I heard you were sick."

"I am."

He was. Clearly so, his voice far deeper than usual. From the faint flush in his own cheeks, he might even have a fever. Guilt flooded me. So he hadn't been avoiding me after all.

"I baked you something, to wish you well," I said with a smile, forcing it to sound effortless.

"You came here to give me cookies?"

"Yes. I live just down the street, as you know."

"Right. Well, come in. I don't..." He ran a hand through his hair, clearly flustered. Thanks to his T-shirt I could see his arms, well-muscled and fair. I'd always been aware of the fact that he was well-built under his tailored suits—had known it, intellectually—but seeing it was completely different. It made me ache for the feel of them around me.

"The kitchen is just through here if you want to drop them off." Grant's voice sounded painful. By the box of tissues I saw on the granite countertop, it was obvious he had the flu.

"I'm sorry for barging in on you like this." I looked at the cookies, avoiding his gaze. "I hope you like them."

"I'm sure I will. Thank you. No one has ever done that before."

"Probably because you're so seldom ill." I gave a small smile, relieved that he was playing along.

Grant smiled back. "That's probably why, yes. It's difficult, being so perfect."

"Naturally, I can empathize," I said and looked past him through the wide archway into a living space. The windows beyond it confirmed what he'd once told me, and I moved past him.

"You told me you had the same view. This is beautiful."

"You remember?"

"Of course. I wasn't that drunk, you know."

"No. I suppose not."

Central Park opened up before us, slightly snow-covered in the dappled afternoon sunlight despite it nearly being the end of February. His windows were far more Art Deco than mine, all clean lines and harsh surfaces. I ran a hand over the smooth leather of one of the large sofas and surveyed his place. There was a second floor, an alcove really, though huge. I could see the edge of a bedspread.

Must be his bedroom.

A TV and a fireplace centered the large living space downstairs. Walls were white, color sparse, and on the walls hung large pieces of abstract art.

"Contemporary," I said. "I would have thought you were a fan of the Old Masters."

Grant gave a shrug. "I am, intellectually. But I can't be surrounded by all that grandeur at home too."

"You prefer new and in disarray?" I smiled.

"I do. That's a Jackson Pollock." He pointed to a piece right by the spiral staircase, a beautiful mess of blues and beiges. "I'll probably sell it when the market is right."

So things didn't have a sentimental value to him, then. It didn't surprise me, seeing the sparse coldness of his home. Decorated by someone who had only the bare necessities in mind—a place should be beautiful, efficient, well-made. And that was that.

"Why'd you really come here, Ada?"

There was something in his eyes and the deep tenor of his voice that made it impossible to lie or flirt my way out of it. I didn't think he'd buy it, and I couldn't bear to see him look through me again, as if he was disappointed that there wasn't more to me.

The truth, then. I took a deep breath. "I was afraid that you were avoiding me, after what happened. First the trip, and then you were sick…"

"I wasn't. Not everything this week revolved around us. The trip was a last-minute thing, but for a long-term client who had sudden needs."

Us. He'd called us an *us.* "Of course. It was a silly fear, but not one I could entirely get rid of."

He leaned back against the couch, both hands in the pockets of his slacks. No one should be allowed to be that handsome while sick. "I can get that. Nothing to fear, though. We're good, just as we discussed earlier."

"We're good," I echoed, thinking of how his mouth had felt on mine only a week earlier. On *me.* This had been a bad, bad idea for my self-control.

Perhaps he realized what I'd been thinking, because Grant's eyes suddenly trailed down to my lips and my neck.

"Thanks for the cookies," he said.

"Don't mention it."

"I'll see you on Monday."

"Yes. If you're feeling well enough to come to work."

"I will be."

"I'm sure. Now that you have a miracle cure."

His brow furrowed for a moment before it suddenly cleared. "Ah. The home-baked goods. Yes, of course."

"Apply hourly," I said sternly. "On the infected area."

Grant gave a crooked smile, holding the door for me as I pulled on my coat. "As the doctor prescribes."

"Bye, Grant."

"Bye, Ada."

14

GRANT

I spent the following week focused on my job.

Or rather, *focusing*. Because to my great frustration, it was a struggle to bring my mind back to whatever task was at hand and away from silk skirts and quivering legs and rosy kisses. Or worst yet, flushed cheeks and shy smiles and offerings of home-baked fucking *cookies*.

What made matters worse? That she was sitting in the room outside of my office.

What made them truly awful? That she was Ada Hathaway, and off-limits in about a thousand—no, a million different ways. Seeing her in my apartment shouldn't have been arousing or moving, and it turned out to be both. Despite all reason, I wanted her there again.

And while it had never been a particularly homey place, it had been mine—and now it was forever changed by her short visit and the impossible-to-forget information that she lived about five minutes away.

She had baked for me. I couldn't remember a time when anyone had done that before. It had been very tasty and very physical proof that whatever attraction there was between us was definitely both-sided, and that she had hoped to continue with our friendship. But Ada's friendship was like a fuse, and either way, I knew I would end up burning. We couldn't be romantically linked. And even as friends, she'd want *more*. More personal details, more emotions, more sharing.

I sighed and looked at the open file on my desk. Pictures and records from social services, my birth certificate, the few remaining legal documents my mother had once signed. The statement from the first foster home. I'd only skimmed through it. It's not like I hadn't known what they'd thought about me anyway.

The PI I'd hired to track down any information about my mother had found very little, so far. With each new update, I knew it was time to shut it down. It'd yield nothing of value, and I had no real use for the information anyway. But there was something unfinished about it, and that wasn't something I preferred to leave be.

"Mr. Wood? The event committee is here for your final approval for the Charity Auction ball."

"Send them in."

The annual ball was one of Hathaway's longest standing traditions. The waiting list was long, the families who want to attend many, and the expectations mile high.

"We've chosen a silver theme this year. It's more of a winter-wonderland look—classy." The outside hire we'd chosen for the job looked very pleased, a pencil behind her ear.

"Right," I said. "Terrific. And Sarah? The auction items?"

Sarah leaned forward—thank God for my own staff—and began listing the top ten. "So as you see, the contributions have been very generous, both from private donors and the company. There is no doubt that we'll manage to raise at the very least the same amount as last year."

"I want to surpass it."

"I know. And I think we have a few surprises up our sleeves for that. A few journalists will be there, covering the event as usual. We'll have the red carpet and the photography done in the hallway."

"Sounds good. I'll leave it in your capable hands. Nothing left for me to approve?"

"No, sir."

They left me to my own thinking, which tended to stray these days. Victoria had accompanied me to these things before, but that was months ago. I hadn't asked a woman out or flirted with one since... since Ada started her internship here. Somehow everything circled back to her, like she was the Rome all roads lead to.

Perhaps I should see if Ada was going with anyone. If she was going with a date, there was no way I could show up without one.

I was returning to the executive floor after having lunch with a client (a long, tedious affair, but she'd finally agreed to list with us) when I shared the elevator with the receptionist.

"Sir." She nodded, a large bouquet of white roses in her arms. She had to use both hands to hold the bouquet. She pressed the button for the executive floor.

"Where are you heading?" As far as I knew, nobody had a meeting with administration or reception today. She looked slightly nervous and I felt bad for having phrased it that way.

"These were delivered to Ada Hathaway. Because of security, the deliveryman isn't allowed inside, of course. So I took it upon myself to deliver them."

"Ah." Anger flared through me, sharp and acidic. She was getting flowers. A week after she stood demurely on my doorstep with still-warm chocolate cookies and a face free of makeup.

The receptionist looked frightened by my curt response. I swallowed back my anger and tried a neutral tone.

"Did he say who they were from?"

She shook her head, so I reached across and found the small note attached to one of the roses. Invasions of privacy be damned.

Ada,

You're the greatest treasure at Hathaway's.

Ben.

The card was made out of thick, beige paper and stamped with the gold logo of Jack and Thorn's.

Fury and fear chased one another inside of me, obscuring all rational thought. The door opened and the receptionist exited first, hurrying across the hallway to the open cubicles where Ada's desk was. I followed her closely.

Everyone looked up when we entered and the tapping of fingers against keys stopped.

"For Ada Hathaway," the receptionist squeaked, offered the flowers to Ada and hurried away.

"Thank you!" Ada called after her. Her hair was swept back and she looked young, nothing like the arrogant socialite who had burst in here on her first day. She looked up at me, and for a moment, she seemed surprised. Did she think they were from me?

Then she registered the look on my face.

"Check who it's from," I told her.

She flipped the card over and I saw her lip curl. Jealousy, acidic in nature, nearly took my breath away. Was she *pleased*?

"Wow. The nerve."

"Who is it?" Sarah bent over Ada's shoulder and read the card before giving an indignant scoff.

"How dare he?"

"Why is he sending flowers to you?" I asked.

Ada shrugged. "I assume it's for the same reason he antagonized you at the event two weeks ago. He's new, he's hungry, and he's eager to make sure we know who he is and that he means business."

"Plus he has a death wish," Linda murmured from her corner.

"I think it's clearly meant as a joke," Ada said. "'You're Hathaway's greatest treasure.' I'm clearly not, so it's a play on words in several ways. He must know that we've overtaken them in Old Masters sales again."

He wanted to psych us out, in other words. If I'd disliked him before, it was nothing like what I felt for the man now.

"He's always been flirty, in that combative way. It's clear he thinks it fun because of who I am."

It struck me first then that Ada might find this all awkward, or worse, mortifying. He was essentially picking on her for the sole reason of her last name in the office space where she was trying to make a name for herself.

I cleared my throat. "He's a prick. And if he tries to intimidate or antagonize you in any way, you let me know, okay?"

Ada gave a small nod. "I will."

I turned to leave, but not before I saw the hesitation as she looked around, bouquet in hand.

"What should I do with these?"

"Do you want them?" I asked her.

"No, not particularly."

I held out my hand and she gave them to me with a small smile. "Thanks, Grant."

"Don't mention it."

They made a satisfying sound as they hit the bottom of my wastebasket.

———

It wasn't entirely out of the realm of possibility that Ada would bring someone to the party.

The more the thought struck me, the more of a potential it became. I'd told her that we couldn't continue whatever we had begun in the storage room, and I didn't expect her to wait or try to ask me again. At best, it had been somewhat of an aberration on her part. A desire for the unknown.

I swore and called in Linda, who arrived faster and with a larger smile than I deserved. "What do you need, sir?"

"I'm heading out to my four o'clock in a moment, but before I do, would you mind telling me who from the office will have a plus-one for the Charity Auction?"

She raised her eyebrows. "From the entire company?"

"No. Only executive branch."

"Sarah is bringing her husband, but as far as I know neither Adam nor Ada are bringing anyone along. Nor am I, as you know. Benny is out on his fishing trip."

I gave a nod. "Very well. Thanks, Linda."

"Don't mention it. Why, sir? Shouldn't we?"

"No, I was merely curious. I'm not bringing anyone this year and was wondering what company I'd be in. Thank you for confirming."

Linda left with a small, secretive smile that led me to believe she might not have bought my perfectly adequate explanation. But I knew she had an active imagination.

And very well-tuned intuition.

———

I tugged at the sleeve of my tux and wondered, not for the first time, when the first charity auction would end. First and second courses had been finished, and the properties section of the evening was taking forever. I'd been seated between Elizabeth, our head of European marketing, and Eugene Bilt on my right. It was a place of honor, and one specifically designed because of his very generous donation tonight. But it didn't mean I liked the man.

"We're more than halfway to the goal," Elizabeth said, indicating the ticking screen behind the tux-clad auctioneer on the stage. "A lofty goal, sir, but I believe we'll reach it."

"We will," I replied and slid a sideways glance to the table beside mine. Ada had arrived without a date, which I was endlessly thankful for, but in a shimmering black sheath that hugged every curve. Her hair was a gleaming wave of gold that made her impossible to ignore.

She was seated between two gentlemen, who by all accounts looked smitten by their beautiful and well-connected table partner.

"A ski-lodge in Aspen. Five bedrooms, four baths, designed as a classic Swiss chalet!" the auctioneer called out. Nearly a dozen paddles went up straight away.

"You've been good for the firm," Bilt said to my right. "An industrious influence."

It was difficult to hear him over the excited bidding, so I merely gave him a nod. His patronizing words stayed with me.

"The firm is currently in its strongest quarter in nearly eighteen years. It's positive to see that art and culture continue to be viewed as valuable."

"Well," Bilt said, raising his glass to mine. "For some, at least."

I didn't toast him. "Nearly a third of all of our auctions are won by museums and public art collections around the world."

"Of course, of course. Didn't mean to offend." He laughed faintly, nonplussed by my response. I took a sip of my champagne. I knew I didn't quite fit their expectations, hadn't since I began. It was fine. They didn't need to understand my motives, they just needed to continue supporting the firm.

"Sold! To the woman in silver. A fine purchase, madame. I'm sure you will enjoy many lovely winter weekends in the accompanying hot tub. And that concludes the property section of this annual Charity Gala. We'll return shortly for our final, super-secret, super-scandalous auction. Be sure to bring out the check-books, ladies and gentlemen, because this one is a good one."

Waiters came to clear the dessert and the soft sound of jazz resumed from the onsite band.

"Excuse me, gentlemen, ladies. I'll return shortly." I rose from my table, several others following suit and angling toward the open bar.

Arthur was standing by a table to the side, a forgotten martini in his hand. He nodded when he saw me approach.

"Grant."

"Hello, Arthur."

"Is it just me or do these parties get bigger and bigger every year?"

"It's not just you," I snorted. "They do."

He looked off into the distance, not seeing the crowds. Arthur was usually well-liked and a sought-after dinner companion at these events, much like me, except people generally enjoyed talking to him. He'd been the board member, CEO and major shareholder for over forty years, when push came to shove. This was his world and the clientele had known him for years, both professionally and privately.

"I used to love these events," he said quietly.

I knew what he meant. *Before.* Arthur had changed after Max's death. I took a sip of my drink and considered how to best respond to my former mentor.

I cleared my throat. "Have you spoken to anyone? You know, about Max?"

He turned to me. "What, you mean a therapist?"

"Yes."

Whatever reaction I was fearing didn't come. He looked up at me with tired eyes, almost as if he had taken off a mask. "No. But maybe I should."

"Maybe so."

He shot me an amused sideways glance. "Would you ever?"

I tugged at my collar. He knew me well, after all. "If I felt I needed it, I would."

"Liar," he said, but he took a sip of his martini and didn't say anything else.

"Ada is here tonight," I said, changing the topic to one that would be welcome for the both of us.

"Yes, I spoke with her earlier. She was excited about the secret auction."

"Was she?"

"Yes. Tell me, there's a month left, but how is she handling the internship?"

"Very well," I replied honestly. "She's hard-working."

"I knew she could be," Arthur replied. "Look, I—"

"Ladies and gentlemen! It is now time for the final auction! For those of you who came without a guest or partner tonight, this is your chance. Let's give a round of applause as we welcome out our first round of goods!"

"Oh dear," Arthur said, clutching his martini. "We'd better return to our seats."

I did just that, watching in silence as nearly thirty people stepped onto the stage. The secret auction was people, then. Mildly tasteless, but if it helped us reach the charity goal, then so much the better.

Both women and men stood shoulder to shoulder in beautiful clothing and giggled amongst themselves, elbowing and pointing at the wide crowd.

"Can you believe it?" Bilt hissed to my right. "What scandalous fun!"

The rest of the guests at my table were similarly engaged. Somewhere across the room an onlooker gave a loud hoot of excitement.

"We will start this auction off with the delectable Miss Daisy Rowman. A dance with her this evening will start at a hundred dollars." An elderly woman with coiffed hair, one of the long-standing customers of the firm, stepped forth. She wore a wide smile and gave a wave to the audience, most of whom she was well-acquainted with personally.

"A hundred dollars. Do we have that?"

"A thousand dollars!" Mr. Rowman stood up at his table and waved his paddle high. Nearly in their seventies, they'd been married for over thirty years. Mrs. Rowman pretended to swoon on stage and the crowd let out a laugh.

I smiled. This might actually help us reach the goal.

"Two thousand!" A woman called from the back.

"Two thousand three hundred!"

"Two thousand five hundred!" Mr. Rowman called again, good-naturedly. Everyone was in on it; the rich people in this room all planning on giving sizable donations. But there were many ways to do it, some arguably more fun than others. Sarah and the event planning committee had tapped into something genius here.

"Sold for two thousand five hundred to the gentleman in the third row back! Brilliant purchase, Mr. Rowman."

"And there is no money-back guarantee," Mrs. Rowman quipped from her position on the stage. Laughter rippled through the room as her husband approached and offered her his arm.

"Next up we have a real catch—Mr. Miles Davis. He works here at Hathaway's as a matter of fact, one of our resident experts on vintage wine and whiskey."

Miles looked slightly uncomfortable but flushed, and I smiled wide. He was a reclusive fellow who spent most of his time studying wine labels. I had begged and bribed him with a six-figure salary to leave his flat in the Loire Valley and make his way back across the Atlantic to join Hathaway's. He'd been worth every cent.

I was pleased when several women, and quite a few men, bid on him too. No doubt hoping to pick his mind.

My smile died instantly. Next up was Ada.

Of course she was doing this.

And she'd be the most coveted prize, the child of Arthur and the only Hathaway of the next generation. Not to mention the fact that the light on the stage reflected in every curve of her shimmering dress, making her already beautifully shaped body seem like rippling water.

"Our next item is none other than Ada Hathaway herself! Imagine our joy when she signed up for this. Who wouldn't want to share a dance with Ada?"

She stepped up by the podium and gave a wide smile. I hated it; it was the one she reserved for photographs and functions and people she secretly disliked. I knew, because it had been directed at me once or twice.

"We'll start the bidding at a hundred dollars, same as for every— Oh! And we're already started. A hundred to the gentleman on the far left. What do we have here? Two hundred to the woman in the front!"

Ada was all smiles and bubbly, sparkly personality up on that stage. Several men in the audience were standing, raising their paddles in an intense bidding race and the price went up up and away. It was now in the several thousands.

It was a ludicrous price for one evening, even with the founder's daughter and heiress. Oh, I was sure they'd all say it was for charity—but it was a price many would willingly pay for one of her smiles. The air felt thin. The idea that she might turn those luminous, shining eyes on someone, to lean in and whisper in their ear… They didn't deserve her. None of us unlucky sons of bitches did, and I least of all, but I wasn't about to let her go off with one of them.

At least I had restraint.

"Four thousand dollars to the gentleman in the blue tux," the auctioneer called out, looking delighted at the flurry of interest Ada had caused. The current highest bidder smiled widely at her, his neat hair just lightly flecked with gray.

Creep.

"Five thousand dollars to the gentleman in the back," the auctioneer called, sounding slightly less enthusiastic. I followed his gaze.

No way.

Ben *fucking* Harris. He wasn't invited, and I could tell by the ripple of excitement that rushed through the audience that some recognized him too. This was *Hathaway's yearly Charity Gala*. We could make semi-civil conversation at other times, but not here.

Stay on your side of the trench, man.

Ada gave him a little wave and I thought I might just black out from the adrenaline coursing through me. This was a train derailing, an airplane heading toward the ground, and I could think of only one way to stave off a crash.

I raised my paddle high. "Ten thousand dollars."

The auctioneer gave me a wide, exuberant look. "Ten thousand dollars to the gentleman we have to thank for tonight. Ten thousand dollars, ladies and gentlemen. Do we have any other takers? Anyone willing to bid above the CEO himself?"

I heard murmurs and flurries of movement, but no one spoke or objected. Ada's gaze met mine across the room. I didn't turn to look at Ben Harris. I'd let him know that this auction room is my kingdom.

Ada looked entirely shocked. There was no little wave or wink to me, and I actually preferred this, having surprised her so thoroughly. I imagined I could see the thoughts spinning in her head.

Have her spend another evening with me and see how she liked it.

15

ADA

Grant bid on me.

It was all I could think as I walked down the dais and grasped his arm. His eyes were indecipherable, dark and calm like the surface of a lake, but I could feel the tension in his arm.

Was it because he won? Or because Ben was here?

I didn't think I could bear it if he only bid on me because of Ben, to make a territorial point in this stupid war between auction houses.

"Why is he here?"

"I don't know. He wasn't invited, but I'm sure he's here to stir things up."

We headed toward one of the tables in the back, away from the crowd and the ongoing bidding.

"Don't tell security to throw him out. It'll only make a scene," I warned.

"Don't worry. I won't." Grant drained his glass of champagne. "He may be unprofessional all he likes, but he won't see Hathaway's indulge him in that."

The silence between us stretched on and I was thankful we were away from any prying eyes.

"So what do we do now?"

I laughed. "I'm your prize. You decide."

Grant shook his head. "There must have been some plan. Dancing, perhaps, once the auction is finished."

I looked back, seeing that there were only a handful of people left up on the dais. "I'm sure it will start soon. Or we could slip away if you're tired of all these people."

Grant slid a sideways glance to me. "I don't think that's a good idea."

"You're probably right." I forced myself to keep a light tone, to not be intimidated by our recent strained friendship or the fact that my heart raced from his nearness. "Hey, you haven't thanked me for those cookies."

"Yes I did. Right away, even."

"*Yes*, but you're supposed to mention it later. 'Thank you, Ada, they were delicious. By the way, here's your pan, washed and clean.'"

"They didn't come in a pan."

"You know what I mean."

Grant gave me a reluctant smile, eyes lightening. "I do. Well then. Cue background music?" He cleared his throat. "'Thank you, Ada, the homemade cookies were incredibly delicious. Please fax me the recipe.'"

I laughed, delighted. "And the Oscar goes to... Grant Wood!"

"Thank you," he said. "I'd like to thank my acting coach for getting me this far."

"Your acting coach accepts this praise. Also, faxing?"

"I improvised." Grant shrugged. "Not my best moment."

I loved it when he was silly, partly because it happened so rarely, and because I felt like a child who'd managed to peek behind the curtain at the theater. Seen behind the facade and the stage, to the real-life workings behind.

"Hey, I went to the Japanese Reading Room at the Met."

He turned to me fully. "You did?"

It was the first time either of us had mentioned the late-night phone calls, which felt unreal, almost as if they existed in another dimension, one where we weren't Ada and Grant but just two voices in the dark.

I swallowed. "It was beautiful. Very quiet, like you said."

"It is a reading room, after all. Did you like it?"

"Yes. Though next time I'll bring a book or something. You know, actually do some reading." I'd sat there for nearly half an hour, taking in the atmosphere, reading up about the room on the different notification plaques and thinking about him. Not that he needed to know the last part, of course.

"Now you have to go to Balto's statue."

"I've already been."

"What, really?"

He gave a nod. "I stopped there last time I was out running. Read the sign and everything."

I could picture it. Him in his dark training outfit, his thick hair slightly sweaty.

"And?"

"I can see why you like it."

"Really?"

"It's a bit like you," he said simply. "Crazy, yet makes perfect sense. Come, it's time to dance now."

He swept me into his arms and we moved in tune with the crowd, slow and careful movements. I swallowed the flush of desire that rose up in me at his nearness, his strong arms around me. This was neither the place nor the time for that, not with so many others twirling around us and watchful eyes around.

"You're good at this," I murmured.

"You sound surprised."

"No. You're good at everything."

He snorted softly, but his lips curled in a surprisingly sweet smile. "You know, half of the time I can't tell if you're teasing me or complimenting me."

"Can't it be both?"

He leaned in closer, turning me so that we floated to the

back of the dance floor. "I've never thought about that before."

"Think outside the box, Grant," I said. "I know you can do it."

The music came to a graceful end, and we swayed momentarily, lost in the moment.

It broke as Adam approached us, his steps long. Grant slowed us to a halt immediately and bent so Adam could speak in his ear.

"Good," Grant responded. "Keep me informed of any changes."

Adam nodded and gave me a brief smile before hurrying back to his date. I raised an eyebrow.

"Ben Harris has left," Grant informed me.

"Without security's assistance."

"Without it." He was quiet for a moment, and we swayed gently on the floor. "Well, I might have sent Elizabeth over there to talk to him, though."

I laughed. "She can be fierce when she wants to be."

"I was counting on that."

"Hey, I was thinking. Have you talked to everyone here?"

"Yes."

"And the goal of three million has been reached." I tilted my chin toward the ticking scoreboard on the corner, where 3.46 million dollars shone in big, white letters.

He stopped momentarily. "So it has."

"What was the charity honored this year?"

"The New York State Orphanage Charity," Grant remarked, looking at something over my shoulder. "I introduced it during the opening speech."

"Right. You were great, by the way."

"Well, you clearly seemed to have been paying attention." But he said it with a wry smile and that sly look in his eye, as if we shared a secret. And I supposed we did—that evening in the storage room hung in the air between us, informing our every move despite both of us doing our best to ignore it.

"I was distracted," I said loftily.

"Oh?"

"It had been a long time since I'd seen you in a tux."

Grant looked down at me in raw surprise. I smiled and tried to play it cavalierly. "You can still pull it off."

"You're the one wearing a starlit sky."

I stared at him in wonder. Who was this man, saying things like that? His eyes widened as he took in my expression. "Why are you looking at me like that?"

"You're something else, you know that?"

Grant snorted again, but it was good-humored and soft. "Pot, meet kettle."

"What I was saying was, if you're done, let's get out of here."

He stopped again, and I pulled us away from the dance floor to avoid obstructing the other pairs.

"Ada, I don't think—"

"Just to get some food and talk. You can't really say you want to stay? And you've already spoken to everyone."

"God, yes. More than I wanted to."

"And you paid ten thousand dollars for an evening with me. Let me treat you to Asian takeout and teach you how to eat with chopsticks."

He was quiet for a beat, even as he leaned forward. I could smell the spicy scent of his cologne, see the sharp lines of his tux up close. I didn't think I'd ever been more attracted to anyone in my life than I was to this cerebral, complicated force of a man. Maddening and joy-inducing all at once.

"It might not be a good idea," he said finally, not sounding very convincing, even to himself.

So I touched his elbow. "We're friends now, aren't we?"

Grant looked down at me for the span of an agonizing heartbeat. "Yes. We are. Come, let's get our coats."

The New York air was cold and crisp, carrying the same weight of possibility and life it always had. I didn't think I would ever grow tired of it, of the way it changed endlessly yet always managed to remain the same. New Yorkers marched on. It was all they knew how to do, and surrounded by that steady pace, I had always found the strength to face the next day too.

We walked side by side toward the small Asian takeout place up the street. His arm brushed occasionally against mine.

As if he could read my mind, Grant spoke first. "Did you miss this place when you were away at college?"

"Yes. New Haven is beautiful, and I miss that too, now. But it was small and only filled with people you knew. There was no anonymity."

"No blending in."

"No. And then, there were memories everywhere."

Grant gave a nod. "I can imagine."

There was something about his steady, calm assurance that soothed the knot of pain in my throat. "I'd walk past the ice cream parlor and think about how he'd always order mint chocolate chip, not because he particularly liked it, but because I *hated* it. The track field where he'd run in the mornings. The small college bar where I'd occasionally pick him up after he'd had too many beers."

"Yes. He liked that, didn't he?"

I swallowed the usual defensiveness that rose when anyone criticized Max. It wasn't helpful, for one, and there was no real judgment in Grant's tone. I owed both myself and Max the truth.

"He did. He was always popular and enjoyed spending time with people. He seemed to care in a way that I rarely can, care about everyone. Maybe that makes me sound awful."

"It doesn't."

"Where I was content with a handful of friends, he wanted everyone to love him. And they did. I didn't approve of some of his friends toward the end. They weren't bad people, don't get me wrong. Just… shallow. Focused on more superficial pleasures."

We ducked around a group of student performers, singing outside of a subway stop. Grant reached into his pocket and tossed a twenty into their open guitar case as we passed.

"Always supporting the arts," I said.

He gave a small smile. "Someone has to."

The conversation lulled, a small breather in the story I was telling. It allowed me to gather strength.

"You didn't run in the same circles, then?"

"Sometimes," I said honestly. "Quite often, as a rule. It's hard not to when you shared a condo, even if we studied completely different things. But I didn't like some of the idiot guys he hung out with, so I often stayed home when they started going out."

"How'd it happen?"

"You must know?"

Grant looked at me steadily, a calm island in a sea of storms. "I do," he said. "But I haven't heard it from you."

And I hadn't told it to anyone in a long, long time. I'd quit therapy after the second time because of all the incessant poking at wounds. But maybe it was time to try again.

"He'd gone out for drinks with some of the boys. It was a normal Thursday evening, nothing special. I'd had my nose in a book on Botticelli, of all painters, because I had an essay due two days later. 'Don't strain yourself now, Ada,' he called to me before the door slammed behind him. He always did that, slammed doors. As if he had too much energy to be contained."

I swallowed, playing with one of my rings, turning it around and around. We'd slowed in our walk, a snail's pace in a city moving a mile a minute.

"He took our car, the one Dad had given us for our twenty-first birthday. We shared it, but we lived by the school and didn't really need it much. Max used it most of the time. I'd told him off for driving when he'd had too much to drink before, but it didn't happen often. He'd shrugged it off and promised not to do it again."

My breath was coming fast; I could feel the pain and tears clawing their way up my throat. Grant didn't say anything. Somehow his calm, steady presence made it possible to continue.

"I was listed as his emergency contact in his phone. A paramedic called me just after midnight."

Is this Max Hathaway's sister? an authoritative voice had asked, and dread had gripped its claws in me.

"I learned later that he had died on impact. I think they expected that to soothe me somehow, make it easier. *At least he didn't suffer,* one of the nurses said. *At least.* As if that made it better. What did it matter, if he'd died in a minute or in twenty? He was twenty-one years old and gone, just like that, snuffed out *on impact.*"

We had stopped entirely. Grant reached up and touched his fingers to my cheek; they came away wet.

I swallowed. "Sorry."

"Don't apologize."

"Our father shut down immediately. I don't think he processed it. I don't think he could, for a long time."

"I'm not sure he has now."

I didn't really hear Grant, memories swallowing me up. "Do you know what he said? 'Thank God he didn't kill anyone.' I know what he meant. But it hadn't even been twenty-four hours yet. I lost it in the emergency room. He killed *himself,* I remember screaming. *What could possibly have been worse?*"

I shook my head, trying to escape the feelings threatening to resurface. I'd lost my family that day, the last tether. Dad was doing the best he could without Mom by his side, but it had never really been enough.

Grant put his arm around me. "I'm sorry," he said. "Truly."

"Thanks."

"Come on," he said. "The takeout place is just up ahead. Pork and Moos, right? I have chopsticks to master."

I gave a small, shaky laugh as we crossed the street. There's something special about people who can listen to difficult things without becoming awkward or uncomfortable. So many of my friends had shied away after Max died, unable to stand my grief. They'd say *I'm sorry* after bringing up anything death-related, afraid to trigger my sadness. As if it was possible to remind me about something I carried with me every minute of every day. The worst had already happened. *You're allowed to use the word dead,* I'd once said to a childhood friend. *That's what he is, and no pretty euphemism in the world can undo that.*

She'd stopped calling after that, and I'd found other ways to numb the pain.

Grant didn't shy away. He just steered us to a corner table and asked the waiter for menus and a large bottle of sparkling water.

"What did you buy for us last time? When you brought it to the office?"

"Red curry and Pad Thai."

"Right. The Pad Thai was good. I'll have that again."

I smiled as I perused the menu, eyes unseeing. Spending time with him could be effortless. It had been a long time since it had felt that way with anyone. "So adventurous."

"Only when the adventure is worth it."

I bit my lip to hide my smile as the waiter came over. Grant ordered first before the waiter turned to me with a wan smile. "And for you, miss?"

"I'll have the entire taster menu and a packet of the dried mango chips. Could we also get four pairs of wood chopsticks, please? The whole thing is to go."

"To go?"

"Yes. Thanks a ton."

The waiter nodded as he scribbled it all down on his notepad, probably used to far weirder orders than mine at this hour. Something about this place, with its slightly broken tile and flickering fluorescent lighting, calmed me. You knew what you got here.

"To go, Ada?"

I gave Grant an angelic smile. "Yep. We're heading to my apartment."

He looked at me steadily, reproach clear in his eyes, but he didn't say anything.

"I need supplies for the lesson. Besides, you don't really want to sit here and learn, do you?"

Grant glanced around. People in various stages of drunkenness were angling in and out and we'd already been given a couple of speculative looks because of our fancy dress. No doubt someone would strike up a conversation if they saw Grant in his tux and powerful air trying to maneuver noodles on two sticks.

"I see your point," he said wryly. "Fine."

"Good. Now, it's your turn."

"My turn?"

"I told you something that was personal. Tell me something."

"It's not a trade, Ada."

"Why not? We're friends, aren't we? How about you say something about your family. It can be anything, any little detail. Doesn't have to be revolutionary."

Grant leaned back on the faded red pleather and looked thoughtful. He would refuse, but there was nothing lost by trying. Seeing if it was possible to peek behind the curtain one more time.

"My mother was a brunette," he said finally.

"Like you, then."

"Yes, I suppose."

"Was?"

"She's gone now."

I stroked the edge of the table, where the linoleum lining had begun to peel off in curled ridges. "Mine too."

"I suppose there are better things one might have in common."

I gave a small smile, careful not to do anything that might shock him out of this new intimacy blossoming between us. "Was your father a brunette too?"

Grant's response, when it came, was measured. "I don't know. I never met him."

"Here, miss, sir. One Pad Thai, one red curry, a full taster menu and dried mango chips." Two white plastic bags were deposited on our table, the outlines of boxes just barely visible inside.

Grant reached for his wallet but I stopped him with a raised hand. "I said my treat, right? It's all part of the evening you paid for."

Too late, I realized what my words sounded like. The waiter's eyes widened. A giggle escaped—I couldn't help it— and very soon Grant was laughing, too. The waiter accepted my money and hurried away without a backwards glance.

"You have a way with words," Grant said and grabbed the bags.

"I'll never be able to come here again," I said with a playful sigh. "What a pity."

We made our way to the front door only to stop dead. It was pouring outside. The sky had opened up and it rained with such fervor that drops bounced off the pavement and the asphalt, water running in rivulets down the street.

"Shit," Grant swore. "We'll have to wait until it stops. We'll get soaked."

A slow smile spread across my face. There was something about this night, about him, about the fluorescent lighting and the spinning, fragile thing between us.

"Hey. Let's be *adventurous.*" I grabbed his hand and pulled the door open, dragging us both outside and into the downpour.

"You've gone mad!" he called behind me. We stopped at a crossing and I mashed the crosswalk button.

"You know that doesn't actually do anything?"

"You never know!" I grinned, just as cars began to slow to a halt. The light turned yellow, then red.

"Hah! All my doing."

"The all-mighty Ada," he said as we ran up the street. It was abandoned, the rain dissuading anyone from venturing outside. Water splattered under my shoes with each quick step.

"Not much farther now!" Grant said, pulling me around the corner. I laughed. My hand was still in his and giddiness rushed through me, exhilarating and strange.

"I haven't done this in a long time!"

"Run?"

"Been out in the rain."

"Probably because you're mostly sane. Just not always," he remarked. The shoulders of his wool coat were black with wetness. I didn't want to think about our shoes.

"Sanity is overrated. Too much of anything is bad, you know."

"I think that saying refers to things like chips or alcohol, not common sense."

"You're a bore."

"So you've said."

We grinned at each other and slowed to a halt outside my door. Billy was outside, pressed to the building under the entrance canopy, and shot us a horrified look.

"Miss Ada!"

"Hey, Billy. I'm sorry to give you such a fright." I smiled at him as he opened the door for us.

"Thank you," Grant offered. "Have a good evening."

"Likewise, sir, miss."

"Enjoy your pickup game tomorrow!" I called to him.

"I will!"

I pressed the elevator button and leaned against the gilded doors. Adrenaline coursed through me. There was a steady *drip drip drip* of water against the marble tiles, our coats heavy with rainwater.

"You really can talk to everyone, can't you?"

I shrugged. "I suppose. But it's not like I always enjoy it."

"I've noticed." He waved me forward before stepping into the elevator after me. "You're good at faking it, too."

"So are you."

He raised doubtful eyebrows. "Hardly."

I gave a crooked smile. "You're right. Not quite as good as me. But I think you wear a facade a lot."

"Don't we all?"

"That's a cynical way to see it." I fished out my keys from the slightly soggy purse. "But it's probably true."

"I knew you were a realist at heart."

I scoffed and opened the door to my apartment. It wasn't immaculately clean, not by any stretch of the imagination, but I was suddenly really happy with my decision to tidy the past weekend.

"You can put the food on the kitchen table," I told Grant, stalking off to find us clean towels. As I rummaged through my bathroom cabinet I heard the rustle of plastic, the scrape of chairs and then the soft, slow sound of jazz.

He was sitting at my kitchen table, long legs sprawled out before him. Small cardboard boxes littered the table and the smell of warm, Asian food filled the kitchen. He'd unwrapped a pair of the chopsticks and was staring at them like he'd spotted a lifelong enemy.

Grant's thick hair was slicked to his head, clinging in odd patterns across his forehead. I tossed one of the clean towels in his direction, staving off the mad urge to smooth the hair back. "For your hair, Justin Timberlake."

He began fastidiously drying his hair in the methodical fashion I'd forever associate with him, grinning. There was something so boy-like about it—as if he was eight instead of thirty. Grant Wood, in my kitchen, soaking wet and about to conquer chopsticks. It was enough to make me question the laws of nature and the universe itself. Was gravity still even a thing? The laws of thermodynamics?

"Why are you looking at me like that?" he asked as he emerged out of his towel, hair half-dried and messy.

I cleared my throat. "Because you look intimidated. By a measly pair of wooden sticks, at that, Wood."

"Very funny. And I'm not."

"Good choice in music," I added and began toweling my own hair. It would be a mess soon, none of the sleek curls I usually preferred.

"You ordered enough food to feed an army."

"We're going to taste it all," I warned him. "You'll learn better if you can try with a lot of different textures and dishes."

"You are entirely making this up, Ada."

I grinned and took a seat opposite him. "Perhaps. But I'm an auctioneer's daughter. Selling things is what I do."

He raised an amused eyebrow. "You mean *bullshitting* is what you do."

"Same same. Come now. I want you to wrap this around the chopsticks, at the base." I handed him a small rubber band.

He stared at it blankly. "What you mean is, I'm going to start with training wheels?"

"Precisely. Which is why I think you'd prefer *not* to be in public."

"You make my ego sound so fragile," he teased. But he used the rubber band to fasten the sticks together at the base. The whole situation felt surreal, something out of a mismatched dream. Only a day prior I had been thinking that he might not even want to be my friend anymore, and now I was teaching him how to eat with chopsticks using the same method Max and I'd been taught as kids. Life, I guess?

"Then hold them like this... yes, exactly like that. Your index finger on top. And then you... Exactly! Now try eating something."

He carefully picked out a piece of tofu from one of the boxes and maneuvered it into his mouth. I watched in bemused silence.

"And ta-da! You're a natural."

"When does the rubber band come off?"

"When you're comfortable enough to try. Maybe later, or next time."

He gave a low, soft laugh and reached to grab the Pad Thai. "Of all the things to do tonight..."

"Spending time with a friend wasn't what you were expecting?"

Grant paused and looked up me. "No. I suppose it wasn't."

"I think you're a person who doesn't have a lot of friends."

"Thank you." Grant tipped one of the small containers of rice onto his plate, using the chopsticks to help. "You sure know how to compliment someone."

But he didn't sound annoyed, and I laughed. "Sorry. But you know what I mean? I don't either."

"I don't believe that for a second."

"Why not?"

"Because you're you." He waved at me with his chopsticks, eyes bemused. "That hardly needs explaining."

"What?"

"You're Ada Hathaway. You... shine." He shrugged, looking uncomfortable. "And I know enough to know that you have a lot of friends to party with."

I blushed, focusing on opening another box. "You're right. But I would describe very few of those people as friends."

"Then why do you spend time with them?"

"I used to, partly because it was an easy way out. I didn't have to talk about anything difficult. They just... make a lot of noise."

"And drown out the silence."

I nodded, putting my head in my hands. "You can be quite easy to talk to."

"When I'm not being an ass, you mean?"

I grinned. "Exactly."

He shoved one of the boxes away from him. Nearly half of the food was still uneaten but would make for a great lunch. We loaded it into my fridge, companionable silence between us. The soft sound of Ella Fitzgerald crooned out from my speakers. I wondered how he'd found my playlists, and why he'd chosen this one. Nerves danced in my stomach. We were friends now, just like he'd said he wanted.

But everything in my body screamed for more. To see how his silent strength operated, to feel his hands on me again. Kissing Grant was like the first, sweet taste of a drug, ruining you forever for other substances. I didn't know if I'd ever crave anything else again.

"Have a seat on the sofa," I offered. "I think I have a bottle of wine somewhere."

There was a pause and I held my breath, waiting for the rebuff, but Grant only nodded. "All right."

I handed him a glass and sank onto the couch next to him. His long legs reached far under my coffee table and he cut a sophisticated presence in my apartment. It's impossible to forget that a man is wearing a tux. Every time you look at him, it hits you anew. They should be illegal.

"Grant?"

"Mmm?"

"Why did you bid on me tonight?"

He spun the wine around in the glass, watched it swirl. "Because of Ben Harris and Jack and Thorn's."

My stomach sank. Of course. Everything for the good of the company, always. Company first. I put the glass down, hating the sudden and completely irrational flood of embarrassed tears in my throat. I'd pressured him to come here and learn *chopsticks* when all he wanted, like always, was to be professional.

"And…" He trailed off and pinched the bridge of his nose in frustration. "It's not an honorable feeling."

"What isn't?"

"Jealousy. I couldn't stand the idea of *him* spending time with you. Of anyone, really, but especially someone who was so hell-bent on courting you because of your last name."

I swallowed. "I thought you only wanted to be friends."

"So did I," he said. "Or rather, I always knew that was what was best."

"Because of the company?"

He was quiet for a beat. "Yes," he said finally. "Because of the company."

"I won't work there forever." I inched closer on the sofa until our shoulders brushed, our knees touching. "And Grant?"

"Yes?"

"Even if he would have won, I'd have never shown him Pork and Moos. And I would *never* have taught him how to use chopsticks."

Grant's lips curved into that gentle, amused smile that I felt was reserved entirely for me. "I'm honored."

He was so close I could feel the heat radiating off him and see the flecks of hazel in his eyes. I reached up and ran a hand through the still damp curls of his hair, thick through my fingers. I didn't think he was breathing.

"I haven't been able to think about anything else but you, not since the storage room," I murmured.

"Me neither. It's been bad for my productivity." He smoothed my hair back, moved closer, and then he was kissing me.

Hot, feverish touches of his lips and tongue, leaving me gasping for more. His fingers trailed over my bare arms, the curve of my neck, the skin of my back. Everywhere he touched I burned. What had been growing between us for weeks was unleashed, and I feared we might combust in the process.

I tugged at the silken lapels of his tux and he shrugged out of the jacket with ease, strong arms wrapping around me.

"Come here," he groaned and pulled me across him. My knees settled on either side of his thighs as we kissed with frenzied desire. It was the storage room all over again, the tempest, the inferno.

His body was hard where I was soft, unyielding as I melted across him. A hand smoothed the spaghetti strap of my dress down my shoulder. Goose bumps raced across my skin.

His tongue skimmed my lips and left me breathless. We kissed and kissed, seeking further and deeper, as if our bodies could become one despite the layers of clothing between us.

My hand slipped down his shirted front, tracing buttons, until it settled on the hard bulge in his suit pants. No way this was going to be one-sided tonight, as it had been last time.

Grant broke off the kiss and leaned back. We looked at one other as the aching tension built between us. The decision was forming in his eyes—I knew it was already clear in mine what I'd chosen.

"Where's your bedroom?"

I pointed my chin to the oak door behind us. "Over there."

His hands cupped my behind as he rose in one fluid moment. I wrapped my arms around his neck and traced the hard line of his jaw as he carried us into my bedroom.

Grant put me down on the bed with sensual slowness and stretched himself out on top of me. I traced him with eager hands and tugged at the buttons of his shirt, my body aching for the feel of skin against skin. He smiled against my lips and kissed me thoroughly. I had expected Grant to be as meticulous and detailed in his lovemaking as he was in his work. But I wanted him wild—I wanted him to lose control. I twisted with my leg around his hip and rolled us around until he was beneath me, strong and masculine against my body. I kissed my way down his chest, opening one button after the other.

"No thinking tonight." I watched him as I slowly unbuckled his belt. Grant's eyes were so dark with desire that they were nearly black, watching my movements.

I freed his erection and cupped him in my hands, stroked and caressed, felt him quiver against me. Stretching out across his body while I continued my ministrations, I tasted every part of him I could reach. His neck was salty under my kisses.

"No more," he groaned. "I can't. Ada."

With a powerful move he flipped us over and tore, actually *tore* at my dress until I was as bare as him. Strong thighs settled between my legs, arms lifted me up and closer.

Grant bent and took my nipple in his mouth. Fire raced through my body, to and from my core, where the need for him ached.

"Please," I murmured. "Grant, no more teasing."

He smiled down at me as his finger played over my core. "Oh, but baby, that's what we do best."

Grant entered me with excruciating slowness, inch after inch, until I clawed at his shoulders for more speed. He shuddered as he finally sheathed himself to the hilt, a strong weight inside me. I felt his heart beating rapidly against my chest and my own breath came in pants.

I wrapped my legs around him and touched my lips to the hollow of his throat.

"Yes," he ground out and began to thrust. Nobody moved like him, and there had never been anything like us together before. He fit perfectly and with each departing stroke I ached for him to return.

The heat built between us, our bodies turning slick with the force of our lust. His hair was silky in my fingers, the skin on his back taut over wide muscles.

"Ada," he murmured against my lips "*Ada.*" His hands on either side of me gripped the sheets.

"Yes." I arched, the force of his movements rubbing against my clit. "Just like that…"

Grant gave a low growl and pulled me closer—there was not a single part of us that didn't touch. It was a fusing, something so powerful and overwhelming that I knew there was no thought to it. As if all pretense had fallen away, all lies and every facade, and there was only us—alone and naked in the darkness, magic created between us.

"Hell, Ada," he groaned above me. I clasped his neck and kept him close as my release barreled through me. It started deep within but soon spread through my limbs, a sluggish and wonderful warmth. Dimly I felt him cry out against my neck and shudder into me with the force of his own orgasm.

"Wow," I murmured into his ear, a dark and damp curl tickling my nose. There was a low chuckle from where he lay, head in the crook of my neck.

"Yeah. *Wow*."

16

GRANT

The numbers on the spreadsheet swam before my eyes as I struggled to refocus. I had a meeting with new suppliers in less than ten minutes and hadn't finished reading through the briefing material yet. There was no reason for this unusual delay in my usually planned days—except, of course, for a five-foot-eight blonde heiress sitting twenty paces outside the door to my office.

Foolishly, I had thought that spending the night with her might soothe the ache that had grown between us. Put the fire to rest, douse it, satisfy us both.

Instead, it stirred within me a desire to be consumed entirely by her flames. A madman, that was what she had made out of me. Delirious and desirous.

And now she was trying to *kill* me.

Ada had worn a skin-tight gray suit, hugging every curve and indent of her body. She looked professional, no doubt, but also absolutely delectable. When I'd seen her on my way into my office, her hair had been up, but a tendril had escaped, curling down the nape of her neck. My hand ached to reach out and trace the soft skin there.

I won't work here forever, she'd said. That was arguably true. She only had a month left of her internship.

I looked down at the papers on my desk only to see Ada before me. My hands on the curves of her hips, a perfect handhold. Her little sounds of pleasure when I first entered her, as if she had never been so gladly surprised by anything in life. And her sweet, satisfied smile after she completely wrecked me, like she couldn't wait to do that again.

There had been no planning with Ada. I had tried to use my usual tricks, my ways of leading that the women of my past had appreciated, but Ada would have none of it. I simply couldn't be in control around her. Not of my own emotions, and certainly not of my libido.

Worst was that she had curled up against me afterward and fallen asleep like that, her face peaceful in slumber. Her hair a golden mess across my chest, and *I had enjoyed it*. I'd slept better than I had in years.

The static in my desk phone crackled, signaling that Linda was about to speak. "Mr. Wood? Your one o'clock is here. Shall I send them in?"

I rubbed a hand over my eyes. "Yes, please do."

I'd just have to make things up as I went along, clearly. It was becoming a common approach these days.

———

An impromptu email from advertising later and then the entire marketing team sat before my desk. They were generally the ones I considered a necessary evil—expensive, difficult, creative—and absolutely essential for the longevity and survival of Hathaway's.

Only this time, they were sitting there with Ada.

"I know this was on short notice, Grant, but I think we could really be on to something," Marc said. "The original idea came from Ada, and then we've refined it and worked on it."

One of the junior marketing associates lifted up a set of thick posters plastered on cardboard.

"These are prototypes," he said and flicked through them. Promotional posters. The *Hathaway's* elegant black and white logo, but displayed like the Hollywood sign on the side of a mountain. Beneath it were drawings of old cars and palm trees.

A Hathaway's Hollywood Themed Auction Party, the subtitle read.

The next displayed Hathaway's logo blazing behind an English country house manor. Ladies and gentlemen in tuxes and wide empire dresses loitered before it. *A Hathaway's Regency Themed Auction Party,* the subtitle read.

They were beautifully made, artistic and elegant with a touch of fun. They offered the suggestion that we didn't take ourselves too seriously while being entirely in on the joke.

Marc rubbed his hands together, eagerness showing in every pore. "Hathaway's stands for trustworthiness and refinement. We don't want to change that—we just want to show that we also know how to have a fair bit of fun. Those who sell most with us will all get invitations to these events. They become something more than just the Charity Auction ball, new events to organize their social calendar around."

"And to increase the social capital of the brand," I added. "To make it more a matter of prestige to list their artifacts and paintings with us."

"Precisely. We play on what we have in spades—the power of our brand," Marc said. "Each auction party will have a different, elegant theme in keeping with the goods we sell that night. Maybe four times a year, or once a season?"

"It's a good idea. If we coordinate with our event team, we should be able to have the first of these events in late April. Is that feasible for your department?"

Marc gave an enthusiastic nod. "It is. We can have further prototypes drawn in and talk to Event."

"Great. Let's schedule a meeting for next week to go over themes more in-depth. We'll need to stockpile certain goods for selling for these events in line with that."

"Yes. And I'd like to reiterate, sir, that Ada was the brain-child behind this entire idea. Credit should go where credit is deserved, don't you think?"

"Quite," I said. Ada had her hands crossed in her lap and looked at me serenely. Nobody who saw her would guess what we'd been doing only hours before.

"We'll leave you to yours, and get in contact with Linda to schedule a meeting next week."

"Until then," I said. The junior associate carefully picked up the prototypes again. They began to make their way to the exit, Ada trailing last. I tried, and failed, to avoid ogling her body from behind in that ass-hugging suit.

She stopped and turned, hitting me with a charming, wide smile. "I was wondering, sir, if we could have a meeting where we evaluate how my internship is going?"

I struggled for composure. "You're requesting an evaluations meeting?"

"Yes. I'd like to see what you think I've been doing right or wrong."

"Come see me after four. I should have a few minutes free."

She gave a brilliant smile. "Will do. Thank you."

One after one they filed out of my office until the door closed and I was once again alone with my books and work and thoughts. I'd prayed she wouldn't do anything stupid now that we'd slept together, nothing that would start rumors flying or tongues wagging. If she wanted an evaluations meeting, I'd give her one—she couldn't simply use it as an excuse to get alone time, even if my heart had leaped at the notion.

I tried to still it.

———

Ada slipped into my office at four sharp, a notepad tucked against her chest.

"Hey," she said.

"Hey."

She smiled slyly and sat down gingerly in the chair opposite me. Was she sore? The question hovered on my tongue—I wanted to know everything about her—only to be quickly killed. *Professionalism, Grant, while in the office.*

"An evaluations meeting, Ada?"

"Yes. We haven't had one yet."

"An oversight on my part, I assure you."

"So? How have I been doing so far?"

I side-stepped the question, asking something that was at the forefront of my mind. "You're an executive intern. Why were you working for Marc's marketing team?"

"I sat next to him at lunch the other week, and we spoke. I shared my idea for it and he liked it. I only participated once more, in creating the design outlines for the poster prototypes to show you."

"You designed them?"

She looked slightly uncomfortable and gave a shrug. "Well, I drew little sketches of how they might look. But they improved them greatly, of course."

"That's quite impressive, Ada."

"Despite not being in the field I'm supposed to work in?" she asked, looking relieved. Did she think I would have objected? Was I that intimidating to her sometimes? Ada seemed completely irreverent most of the time. She certainly had in bed.

"You're an intern. You're here to learn and to contribute. This was a terrific contribution that didn't distract you from your other tasks. I'd say it shows initiative."

She blushed. "Thank you. I know you're not a fan of events, Grant, but with Jack and Thorn's competing in commission fees I thought we could hit them with glamour. That's what Hathaway's is associated with, anyway."

And you, I wanted to add. Built upon your family's charm and wealth.

"Yes."

"Would you like to do more of that in the future? Marketing?"

"Maybe. It's interesting. Although I think the design part is more what I enjoy."

"Good to know."

"So? How have I been performing?"

I couldn't help but smile at her eagerness. She really did want an evaluations meeting, then, and not just an excuse to spend time privately after last night.

Somehow, I felt both pleased and disappointed by that.

"Very well. Adam and Sarah both consider you a contribution to the team, and I know that Linda is very pleased with your assistance in handling the mailbox and scheduling. Your work with Marc shows initiative and creativity."

She gave a small smile. "That's good to hear."

"What do you want to do with your final month of the internship?" The *final month*. The implication was clear between us, and I saw in her gaze that she understood. Only one more month until I was officially no longer her boss.

"Continue as I have. Perhaps rotate down and see some of the divisions in action that I haven't before."

"Excellent. Talk to Sarah about that—you should be able to accompany either her or Adam on visits, or me, should there be one you see in my schedule that seems interesting to you."

"Thank you." Her smile shifted from a kind one to one tinged with intimacy and secrets. "And thank you for last night, Grant."

The door was closed. My com was off. No one would hear —and at the moment, I hardly cared if they did—as long as she kept looking at me like that.

"Sore today?"

Her eyes widened in surprise and then her smile turned fully wicked. "A little. You?"

I laughed. "My shoulders ache."

She eyed her nails. "I'm not sorry."

"Me neither." I considered her. "No regrets, Ada?"

"None at all." Her eyes were warm. "I take it you don't have any either?"

"No. Only one month left..." I said, letting the statement trail off.

"Yes. But that doesn't mean we can't spend time together out of the office."

"It's not a good idea," I said, but it wasn't in negation. Just a statement of fact, one I knew that neither she nor I could possibly fulfill. I wanted her again. Hell, I wanted her now, here, in my place of work.

She cocked her head slightly and pursed her full lips. "Is that really what you want, Grant?"

"No. It's not. Come over to mine tonight. Around eight. I'll order some dinner for us."

"Sushi," she said immediately. "So you can practice."

Irrational warmth spread through my chest at the thought, just as anticipation curled in my stomach.

"Sushi," I agreed.

17

ADA

The bed was empty when I woke, the room dark. The clock only read 3:40—we'd gone to bed around midnight, after sushi and drinks and a fairly unreal evening. There was something about seeing Grant at ease that would never grow old. His eyes soft and warm with laughter, his shirt unbuttoned entirely... it was quite a sight.

So where was he?

I rolled out of bed and pulled on my robe. My hair was tousled from the sex we'd had before falling asleep and my skin smelled faintly of his cologne. We were in his apartment this time so he couldn't be far.

I walked out of his bedroom on quiet feet in search.

It wasn't hard to find him.

Grant was silhouetted against the Manhattan skyline, sitting straight and quiet on a futon with his back to me. He couldn't have heard me come in, because he didn't turn, only continued to stare out across the city like a man deep in thought.

There was something so profoundly lonely about the tableau that I pulled my robe tighter around me.

Grant glanced my way. "Oh. I'm sorry. I didn't mean to wake you."

"You didn't." I took a seat next to him.

His muscular thigh was hard next to mine, warm through the robe. He was only wearing a T-shirt and boxers.

"Couldn't sleep?"

Grant shook his head slightly. "No. The city is beautiful at night, though."

"It is." I took a hold of his hand and played with the fingers lightly. "Do you have bad dreams sometimes?"

"Occasionally." He turned to me, breaking the stark line of his profile against the light. "Why?"

"I did. For a long time. They're less frequent now, but it's still as jarring when they happen."

He was quiet for a beat. "I can imagine."

"You know you can tell me things as well, right?" I said tentatively. "Like I told you about Max? If you want, I mean."

His hand tightened in mine. "Why are you saying that?"

"Because I care. And because I feel like you might not have that many people to confide in."

"Why do you think I need to confide in someone?"

There was no menace to his questions, no anger, only soft inquisitiveness. As if he could ask things about the way I see him in a way he never would during the day. The night put, as always, a damper on things—covered it all so that only the brightest of things could shine through.

It lets us see clearly.

I shrugged gently. "Only because of things you've told me. That your mother's gone, for example. And that the yearly Charity Auction was changed to focus on orphanages the same year you began."

His hand grew taut in my grasp. "You've been doing your research."

I smiled, a little sad, and tried to look encouraging. "Not really. Just listening."

He was silent for a long time as we watched the city below and from afar, removed from the hustle and bustle on the streets. Somehow there was never a dead moment in New York.

"I didn't know it was possible to see so much," he said finally.

"Only when you stop and look. But it's not something I think you have to hide."

"No," he said. "Perhaps not."

An arm came around me, strong and firm, pulling me into the warmth of his side. Lips touched my forehead.

"Come, Ada. Let's go back to bed."

———

Being in the office the next day felt like being in school, carrying around a secret so big you felt like you might just burst with it.

The fact that Grant was nearby permeated everything I did, every thought I had. To think I'd once dreaded coming to work *because* of him.

The papers for the day's meeting were neatly stacked on my desk, delivered by the overnight courier. I grabbed them and my coffee cup, ready to head to the briefing meeting when Sarah burst into the office.

"Gosh, I'm so late."

"Not to worry." I smiled. "Nothing major has happened. You're only an hour later than usual."

She slung her bag over her office chair and shook red hair out of her eyes. "Yeah, but it's an hour that counts. Did you hear?"

"Hear what?"

"One of our biggest clients just dropped us for *Jack and Thorn's.*"

"Oh no. That's the worst."

"It is." She nodded. "Not that we don't take their clients, but that doesn't make it easier when it happens to you." She rubbed a hand over her forehead. For a moment I was glad I wasn't in charge of customer relations—and had to report to Grant.

I put the stack of papers down. "Hey, whatever you need, let me help. Just give me instructions and I'll be off."

Sarah smiled wanly. "Thank you. I'll let you know in an hour when I have a good overview of the situation."

"All right. I'll be back from my meeting then."

She stopped me with a hand to my elbow. "You look great today. Have you done something different?"

"No."

"Are you sure? Nothing with your hair?"

I fiddled with my bracelet and smiled. "Nope. Just a good eight hours of sleep and all that."

"Right." She smiled. "See you later."

I smoothed a hand over my hair as I hurried away and smiled to myself. We had *definitely* not gotten eight hours of sleep last night.

And I hadn't fallen asleep again right away after our discussion either, instead thinking about what little he'd said and the document I'd found that fateful day in his office weeks ago.

Graham Woodhouse, fostered by the Eltons. He'd been eleven in the photo. Was he ever adopted? I knew that for a lot of older children, the prospects were very slim. Curiosity and a desire to unlock his secrets blossomed in me, despite my own admonitions. But whatever he wished to share with me would have to be in his own time.

That didn't mean that I couldn't do some of my own amateur sleuthing, however. Time to call in the big guns.

"Hi, Dad!"

There was a faint pause on the other end of the line. "Hi, Ada. To what do I owe the pleasure?"

"Just wanted to catch up. How's the Hamptons?"

"It's good. The trees are starting to spawn leaves. I think it might be possible to put the boat back in the water soon. It's high time, too. She's been missing the ocean."

"I'm sure she has," I said sympathetically, thinking that the sailing boat *Marie* likely wasn't having any kind of sentient thoughts. "And you're eating well? Taking care of yourself and everything?"

"Yes, yes, of course." Faint pause again. "Are you?"

"I am."

"The internship still working out?"

"It is. I'll admit that I'm really enjoying it here, more than I thought I would."

"I can't tell you how much that pleases me to hear. Only a little while longer now. Do you know what you want to do afterward?"

"I have some plans," I said evasively. "But Dad, can you tell me where Grant came from when he first started working for you?"

"Where he came from?"

"Yes. Was he working somewhere before?"

"Oh, no. Not that I know of, though I'm sure he was." He gave a fond laugh. "He showed up at my office, knowing everything about the company. Ideas right off the bat for improvements, suggestions, all kinds of things. What else could I do but hire him?"

"No resume or anything?"

"I didn't even ask for one. You don't get too many people like that."

"Hmm. Thanks."

"Why do you ask?" Amusement suddenly colored his voice. "Don't tell me you two are actually getting along?"

"Grant is a good boss," I said. "I was just curious, seeing that no one knows anything about his past."

"Oh, well he doesn't talk about that."

"No," I ground out. "Clearly."

"Thanks for the call, Ada."

"Yeah. Hey, are you coming down to Harry's retirement party tomorrow?"

"Yes. I couldn't very well miss it—I once hired him!"

"See you tomorrow then."

"Will do, Addie."

He hung up. I looked out at the skyline and considered his words. Grant was secretive with everyone then. Even with my father, whom he had followed around for years before he was given the reins to the company. He'd just have to share that part of him with me whenever he was ready.

I hoped I'd be ready to hear it when he did.

18

GRANT

Work was good. It was *safe*.

Because when I was in my office I couldn't see a blonde, bouncy ponytail or a curve-hugging dress. I could bury myself in paperwork and focus only on sales, emails, phone calls, and clients.

The magazine in my hand was glossy with embossed letters on the front. Ben Harris's charming, clean-cut, smug face smiled up at me from the cover. He was leaning against a desk, legs crossed, a vintage-looking globe next to him. It was turned to show Europe and Africa. I leaned in closer, using the set of spyglasses I kept on my desk.

Yep. It was small, but East and West Germany were clearly marked on the map.

Hah. Not even an antique. Only a cheap knockoff from the late 1900s, made to look old. No self-respecting auctioneer would pose with such an item.

Art Weekly was the premier magazine amongst the Manhattan elites interested in both purchasing and selling antiques, not to mention people across the Eastern seaboard. And he'd landed a cover and a two-page spread inside, chronicling the life and rise of Jack and Thorn's new CEO.

I'd turned them down twice, because I had self-respect.

So I put the magazine in the trash and returned to my computer. And then I opened my email and wrote one to Jenna Marlon, the chief editor of *Art Weekly*, saying that I now found it an appropriate time in my career to appear in the magazine, should they still want me. And that she was welcome to get in contact with our head of marketing for the issue.

I would make sure Marc insisted on a four-page spread including Hathaway's illustrious history as well.

There were very few things I wouldn't do for this company—I'd be damned if I let Ben Harris beat us.

An email dropped into my inbox that afternoon from Ada. I seldom emailed with her; most of her assignments came from Linda, Sarah or Adam. So it was with a smile that I opened it.

She'd sent me a screenshot of her office calendar, perfectly organized in the same system that Linda used for mine.

FROM: Ada Hathaway
TO: Grant Wood
SUBJECT: Progress report

Dear Grant,

I thought I'd share just how much headway I'm making on my time-management skills, courtesy of my fortune cookie. Can you imagine that I've already finished the book you lent me?

That's how bored I am these days, having nothing to do and no one to spend time with after work... I don't think that's right. Well-arranged time is the surest sign of a well-arranged mind, after all. And my schedule looks depressingly empty this evening.

Will you help me fill it?
/Ada

I couldn't help the smile that spread across my face at that. She was unstoppable. My hands already ached to hold her again, my body not nearly satisfied despite the two nights we'd spent together.

I'd suggest her place this time. Having her at my apartment had been... too intoxicating. Seeing her in my sheets, wandering my bedroom in my T-shirt as she brushed her teeth. There was an intimacy in that, one I hadn't experienced in a long time. She'd curled up beside me, not content in staying to her side. And when I'd pulled her close, she had sighed happily in her sleep, the sound replaying in my head for a long while afterward.

And she'd asked about the orphanage. I knew she was far cleverer than the world had given her credit for, had often been delighted by her quick mouth. Naturally, she would put two and two together. It had been foolish of me to think she wouldn't.

But she hadn't shied away or pried. There had almost been some curious release in talking to her. In hearing her opinions on things, even those that I didn't think about too often. Ada had a strange perspective on the world, twisting and turning things in ways I hadn't considered before.

Was her email a playful way of asking me for my own progress report? My fortune cookie had been about *love.*

No. Ada wouldn't, and she couldn't expect me to respond to that anyway. That was insane.

Or would she?

Whatever we had was quickly moving out of the casual territory I'd been trying to keep it in.

I shook away the thought and typed a quick response.

FROM: Grant Wood
TO: Ada Hathaway
SUBJECT: RE: Progress report

Happy to hear that. It's clear that being in my company has improved you greatly.

And you're correct—empty space in a planner is unacceptable. I have ten minutes free between meetings next Thursday and I'm already stressed by the thought. Of course I'll help you out this evening.

It's a tough job but someone's got to do it.

/Grant

———

I checked my watch. Nearly seven.

I'd made reservations at the small Italian place between our two apartments, a restaurant I'd only ever walked past. Ada had once remarked that it looked like what a cartoon artist might draw if asked to describe Italy—a large replica of the tower of Pisa stood by the entrance, and the tablecloths were all red and white checkered.

Naturally, we had to check it out. If the waiters were all named Giovanni and Paolo she'd likely have a laughing fit. I smiled at the thought. Ada was silly, and kind, and far better than I could possibly deserve. There was no way she'd stick around.

The sound of my cell phone cut through my thoughts.

"Grant Wood."

"Hi, Mr. Wood. It's Thomas."

My private investigator. I sank back down in my office chair. There could only be one reason he was calling this late. "You've found something."

"Your birth mother. The adoption agency didn't have any records, but I managed to talk to the woman on duty the night you were left there. She'd retired since."

"And?" My stomach curled in on itself, despite my earlier

decision that whatever he found didn't matter, not really. I just wanted to know *why* a mother would choose to hand over her five-year-old son and drive away. There'd never been any explanation.

"She said the woman spoke in a Southern accent. She looked exhausted, like she'd driven many hours and across states. When the nurse on duty pointed out you can't give grown children up for adoption, 'you can't just leave him,' she had said, the woman had shrugged."

"What did she say?"

"'I just can't.' That was all she'd said."

And then she'd pushed me forward to the nurse and turned without another word, hurrying out to the still idling car. Yeah, I knew the rest of the story.

"But no follow-up with the lawyers?"

"New York state didn't do a very thorough job," he sighed. "They could eliminate pretty quickly that she wasn't from the state, but other than that, there was no further examination. I'll continue going through birth records across the country and cross-reference that with missing children's reports."

"The odds that anyone reported me would be slim," I pointed out.

"Yes. But it's the best bet we have right now."

"All right. Thank you for calling me with the info."

"I'm sorry, Grant," the voice said on the other end. "I know this might not have been the result you were looking for when we decided I'd follow the adoption agency lead."

"Not to worry. Thank you for tracking this down. Great work. I'll wire you the next check on Monday."

"Take care, Mr. Wood."

"You too, Thomas."

Well then. I guess I had my answer. All she'd said was "I just can't." No big reason, no confirmation—just another dead end. It wasn't much of a surprise, as I'd never really believed she'd had a good reason, and having it confirmed should be good. Nice. Only it didn't feel that way.

Against my better nature, I wanted to share the news with Ada. What would her take be? But I bit down the urge before it even blossomed. Talking about this to someone... impossible. Particularly when I didn't even know what to think about it. And she had more than enough of her own sorrow without needing to hear a word of mine.

I had fought *tooth and nail* to get out of that world, and I would be damned if I let myself get put back in it—even if only in someone else's eyes.

A soft knock sounded on the door. Ada smiled at me, her coat already on. "Grant? Are you ready?"

"Yes. Let's go," I said and flicked off the light on my desk.

———

I woke early, like always. Ada was asleep against me, impossibly warm and close. Her hair was tousled gold across the pillowcase.

Last night had been a dream. If she wasn't naked against me, I might have trouble remembering it had ever happened.

Falling asleep again was hopeless, especially with us both nude. I would never be able to calm down enough to relax. And she needed to sleep.

So I pulled on my suit pants from the night before and gently shut the door to her bedroom, making my way to the kitchen. There had to be breakfast somewhere.

Her place was roomy and comfortable, decorated with the kind of messy—but slightly sophisticated—creativity one might expect from Ada. I smiled at the compilation of art on the far wall. An abstract art piece hung next to a classical portrait of a woman clad in Renaissance clothes. Likely from the 17th century, if the frame was anything to go by.

A bookshelf stood close by. There was no system of organization and no rhyme or reason to their placement. Everything from old art history books to the latest thriller.

I paused at the top shelf and the framed photos that occupied it. A woman with a blonde bob sat behind two smiling children, an arm around each of them. Child Ada had lost both front teeth; Max sported a shirt with superheroes on it.

The photo next to it showed the four of them in front of the Eiffel Tower, Ada and Max both wearing braces. Arthur smiling at the camera, his arm around his wife. I never met her.

The final photo was from their high school graduation. Only Max and Ada were pictured in their robes; Arthur must have been the photographer. Their mother was nowhere to be seen. Marie, I remembered.

She had had a family. Trips, holidays, gatherings and laughter. It pained me that it was taken away from her.

I sank down in the ludicrous velvet couch. Central Park was hazy with fog in the early morning hours, the sun only barely awake. I didn't blame it. I should be asleep too, a beautiful woman in my arms.

She would want that again. Stability, family. A relationship. More than that: she deserved it. A woman like Ada should be adored for life by a man worthy of her smiles.

And I would only dim her shine.

There were plenty of things about my own heart that were a mystery to me. But I knew it couldn't take any more rejection, and especially not from her. And Ada's would be inevitable.

Because she would realize it. Maybe not today, maybe not tomorrow, but one day she'd see just how far below her standards she had reached, when she reached for me.

19

GRANT

Harry's retirement party was a small, intimate event, made all the more fun because of the person honored. Harry from Books and Manuscripts had been working for the company for more than forty years, and I'd commissioned both a placard and an engraved gold watch to see him off as a thank you for long and committed service.

Nearly the entire company had turned out for the free food and a glass of wine, but mostly, I suspected, for Harry.

"The event team has thrown together a great mixer," Arthur said by my side. "This should become the new standard for retirement parties."

I nodded. "It's truly excellent."

Hathaway's lobby had been converted into a large open dance floor and mingling space, tables laden with hors-d'oeuvres. The staff could stop by after work on their way out and spend an hour or two toasting Harry.

"I'm glad you could make it," I said. "I know that Harry appreciated it."

"It seemed so, yes, although he's now bombarded with hordes of loyal followers." Arthur smiled and nodded toward a far corner. "Plus, it gave me a good excuse to come see Ada."

"I don't necessarily think you need an excuse to see her, sir."

He turned to me with raised eyebrows. "No? Perhaps you're right."

Both of our eyes trailed her where she laughed on the dance floor with Sarah. Her hair was gleaming and unbound, an apparition in the otherwise gray environment.

"I'm really glad, seeing her like this. That the internship is working out."

I nodded. "She's been a real asset. I hate to say it, but you proved me wrong."

Arthur exhaled. "I'm not sure you understand just how glad I am to hear you say it. She's lived up to your expectations, then?"

"Surpassed them, I'd say," I responded honestly. "She's shown both initiative and hard work."

"Gosh. I hoped, but... I didn't admit it to you, but I was worried in the beginning, whether she'd manage it."

"I couldn't tell," I said dryly, "the way you sang her praises."

He shook his head with a small laugh. "And had it not been for the threat, I'm not sure she ever would have agreed. Funny, isn't it?"

"Sorry?"

Arthur turned to me, a relieved expression on his face. "I couldn't see her going down that path, Grant. You know. It wasn't... I couldn't. So it was either this internship, or I would cut her off. She needed to impress you and make this work to stay on the family card. I knew how hard you are to impress, so if she managed to get your approval, I'd know she'd earned it fair and square."

I nodded stiffly. My eyes followed her on the far-off dance floor where she twirled along with Sarah, shimmying in time with the beat.

"I can't thank you enough," Arthur continued, seemingly unaware that I had become iron next to him. "You not only took my family legacy and made it your own, but you seem to have set my daughter straight. The Hathaways will never stop being in your debt."

"Don't mention it." I drained the glass of champagne I'd been holding. So that was why she'd been working so hard, then. Staying late and buying takeout and midnight phone calls and making out with the CEO at parties.

Everyone wanted something from me, it was just never *me*.

I'd been a fool to expect Ada to ever want something else. Her words came back to me, whispered to her brother all those years ago. *He's a nobody.*

I'd made my peace with them and with her. I'd reconciled myself to the fact that she'd been sixteen and eager to impress her brother and they were caught up in their own cleverness and immortality.

To find out that all this had just been for continued access to her nepotistic, elitist trust fund felt like a cosmic joke.

I slipped out of the retirement party early, saying goodbye to no one. The walk to my apartment was quick and I briskly changed into my workout gear. Anger drummed in me, hiding just under the surface, an electric current I couldn't seem to unleash. I didn't know what I'd do if I did.

New York was cold and distant as I pounded across the sidewalk and into Central Park. The only sound was that of my feet against the ground, the trees twisted and foreign around me. In the dark, the park transformed away from something I knew like the back of my hand and into a distant wilderness. I could be back in the deep thickets of the forests upstate again, for all I knew.

She would be cut off from the family card if she failed to meet your approval.

The words refused to disappear, even as my lungs screamed and my legs ached from the grueling pace I set. I had run for so long, but it seemed I couldn't outrun Ada *fucking* Hathaway.

She'd texted me the night before.

Ada: Hey, where did you go so fast last night?

Ada: I think perhaps it's time for your third lesson tonight. My place? I'm home around seven.

There was no rational thought in my mind apart from the very simple one: I needed to talk to her. To set things straight and clear whatever misunderstanding there seemed to be between us. To call the bluff, so to speak. So I responded.

Grant: I'll be there.

I pigeonholed myself in my office the entire day, brushing past the executive team when I inevitably had to go to meetings or lunch with a client.

Had everything been a play? Some form of bluff—a hustle? And I'd fallen for it, of course—plied with practiced smiles and beautiful secrets and *I need you, Grant.*

Yeah, she had needed something from me all right, but it surely hadn't been *me.*

The walk to her apartment felt too short and also a million miles long. The doorman gave me a friendly smile and a wave as I entered.

"Nice to see you again, Mr. Wood. I'll send you straight up."

"Thank you," I replied. There was no need for him to look so chipper.

She opened on the first knock, breathless and rosy. "Hey." She smiled. "Come in, come in."

I followed her into the entry, not bothering to take off my coat.

"I've tried cooking this time, though I'm not sure if it will actually turn out edible. We might just have to order in again! But hopefully not." Her voice trailed off into the kitchen and I heard the opening and subsequent closing of the oven. "It smells good at least. I'm making roasted chicken with baked potatoes. Why are you still standing there? Grant?"

"Ada. We need to talk."

One of the oven mitts fell out of her hand. "Oh. Yes, sure. Should we sit down on the sofa?"

"Arthur told me something interesting the other night. That he forced you into this internship with the threat of losing your trust fund, that he would cut you off."

"Yes." She nodded slowly. "That was what he said. The original deal."

"And that the determiner of whether or not you had succeeded was my approval. He seemed relieved when I gave it."

She didn't look relieved at the information, only worried, a furrow in her brow. "He didn't say exactly what metric he was going to use, but I think your good opinion was probably one of them. I'm sure he might also ask Linda."

"So you're not going to deny it?"

"Deny it… Grant?" She swallowed audibly. "I know that the mode of me beginning to intern at the company wasn't exactly honorable. I know that. But I have loved it."

"Setting an evaluations meeting yourself, suggesting things to the marketing team, coming with me to visit Charles Burch…" I shook my head and forced out the words. "Taking me to the storage room during an event. All of it wasn't some elaborate plan to get me to change my opinion of you?"

She sat down on the armrest, hands clasped tightly in her lap. "You're implying that I slept with you to gain access to my trust fund." Anger of her own laced her words. "That's actually what you're doing. I can't believe this."

Put that way, it sounded positively lurid. "I'm *asking* you if that was what you're doing," I said, voice stone. She wasn't denying any of it.

Color rose on her cheeks. "No, you're not. You're accusing. And I think I know you well enough by now to know that you're not going to change your mind because of my words."

I gave an incredulous laugh. "You *kept* it from me, the real reason you did this internship. And now you're offended that I'm angry? That I am capable of drawing the obvious conclusion?"

"I have *never* in my life slept with anyone in search of benefits. What we did was one hundred percent real, Grant, at least from my point of view. I told you things I've never told anyone." Anger and something that sounded dangerously like tears made her voice waver. "But thank you for calling me a whore. You're an asshole, Grant. Please leave."

"Gladly," I said. "And I still expect you in the office on Monday morning."

"Of course!" she called behind me. "Because I take pride in my job!"

The door slammed between us, and the silence spoke only of injured pride, regret and the bitter taste of anger.

20

ADA

I wasn't proud of it, but I spent the evening crying.

It had been months since that had last happened, when I'd had to walk to the corner shop in my great wool coat and ask for a twenty-four-pack of Kleenex. When my eyes had been so red that I knew people would turn and look.

The entire argument replayed over and over in my head, every ugly word examined and repeated. How could he think such a thing? And why hadn't I told him before about Dad's requirement? It had been out of my mind so completely once I'd begun falling for Grant.

The bed felt big without him, despite the fact that he'd only slept in it twice. Abruptly, I wanted nothing more than to change the sheets. I'd already stripped off both pillowcases when I changed my mind and shoved the pillows roughly back inside, slipping into bed instead. The room was dark as I lay staring up at the ceiling. My phone said that it was a bit past one in the morning.

There was so much I should have said.

It was with shaking hands that I dialed Grant's number. It rang for so long that I was certain he wouldn't pick up. Why would he, if he thought that all I'd been doing was using him?

"Ada," he finally said. His voice sounded clear, as if he'd been awake too.

"Can I add something?"

He was silent for a long time. "Yes."

"It's true that the only reason I accepted the internship was because of the ultimatum with my trust fund. I did it because I had to. But that very quickly stopped being the reason. Since then, I have enjoyed every day at Hathaway's. Not a day has gone by where I've regretted the decision. I wanted to earn my place there, both in the eyes of the employees and in yours. And not once, Grant, did I pretend in order to make you like me." I felt the tears hovering in my throat and my voice wobbled precipitously, both with anger and tears. "Your opinion mattered to me. And if you can't see that, then I'm sorry I ever thought so."

There was complete and utter silence on the other line.

"Good night," I said, and hung up.

————

Minna had diagnosed my strong reaction already, of course. Abandonment issues, she'd said in a clear, proud voice. You lost your mother, your brother, and now Grant. Why would you ever want to open yourself up to love if they all leave?

I hadn't even bothered to contradict her or argue, because I was pretty sure that she was right. But that's the thing: being diagnosed doesn't mean you're any closer to the cure.

Symptoms?

Re-runs of *Sex and the City* and an entire batch of Pillsbury chocolate-chip cookies. Even my sad, miserable existence found the energy to put them in the oven and wait twelve minutes for chocolaty heaven.

Somewhere during the past weeks, Hathaway's had crept under my skin and into my blood. The pace and the people, the ever-changing art pieces and the energy of the auction; it all mattered to me now. And I knew I'd miss it when I left.

But what I'd miss the most was Grant. Grant, who held me like I was precious, who raised an eyebrow and challenged me, who had accused me of *sleeping with him* for my trust fund. I'd never been so offended and angry in my life, even if it was clear how it looked. I supposed I'd thought that Dad had explained it all to Grant when he convinced him I should be allowed on as an intern. And then I hadn't given the whole thing another thought, really.

I took a sip of my tea and sighed. My mug hit the table far harder than I'd anticipated, the loud noise startling Minna from her book. "Woah there, angry pants."

"Sorry."

"He still hasn't called, huh?"

"No." It was Sunday, nearly two days after our fight, and there had been no contact between us. No more late-night phone calls, no texts, no surprise knocks on my door. And no letters hand-delivered to my doorman either—because to my chagrin and infinite shame, I'd phoned down three separate times to ask. When Diane in reception kindly informed me the third time that there was no postal service on Sundays *as was common practice*, I knew it was time to stop.

I didn't do moping, and I thought I'd known anger before. But that was *nothing* compared with how I felt after he'd accused me of such manipulative behavior. As if all the touches, the words, had all been an elaborate lie.

"Do you know what I think?" Minna asked.

"What?"

"That you're a little bit in love with him."

I didn't protest—which made it all the more difficult. She might have a point. There was so much Grant in my head that I scarcely had time to think about anything else. "No, of course not. But... do you know what?" I said, covering my head in my hands. "I think I might be heading that way. And he is *clearly* not with me!"

"Do you think he would have accused you so harshly if he hadn't been hurt by the thought?"

"Yes," I objected, stubborn. "It hurts his principles. I don't even know if he has emotions."

"Come, have a seat here," Minna said and patted the sofa next to her. "I think what you need is something good to look forward to. You finish the internship when? The end of March?"

"Yes. And I don't really know what to do after that." I sighed, putting my head in my hands. Something to fill my days with. Once upon a time, I had had so many plans. Perhaps I should try to get back to that, but where do you start trying to piece your life back together? How do you solve a puzzle without knowing what the final image is meant to look like?

"About that," Minna began in a soft voice. "I've been doing some research, Ada, and I have a suggestion—if that's something you'd feel ready to hear."

I slowly lowered my hands and looked at her slightly sheepish expression. "What exactly are you saying?"

She shrugged innocently. "There's this place that my professor spoke about in class. I think it might be great for you."

"In *psychology* class, you mean."

"Yes. But before you say anything—don't look at me like that, Ada—let me show you a website. Promise me you'll actually read it all and think about it for a minute. After that we can never speak about it again, should that be your decision."

I sighed, grabbed my laptop from the side table and sat down next to her on the couch. The computer balanced on both of our knees. Grabbing the bag of chips from the table, I put my hand to my forehead as if I was a long-suffering martyr.

"If you must," I heaved, "then I agree."

———

Another week passed. He was so cordial it hurt; the mischievous glint in his eye or the sly curve of his lips was nowhere in sight. I missed it with an ache that was painful. We hadn't reverted to what we were before—because that had been enemies, people hovering on the border of civility and nastiness and flirting, I saw now. No, now we 'were something far, far worse.

Strangers.

I think even the others saw it.

Minna had no further advice to give, and I didn't ask any, either. But that didn't stop her from coming over nearly every night.

Minna: Let's watch How to Lose a Guy in Ten Days today.

Minna: No, Notting Hill.

Minna: NO I KNOW! Four Weddings and a Funeral!

Ada: Are you trying to make me feel worse?

Minna: I think we need to purge it out of your system.

Ada: You're a weird friend. Also, let's do Notting Hill.

Minna: A fine choice. See you at mine at eight sharp.

Ada: Why sharp? Are we waiting for someone else?

Minna: Hugh Grant's jawline waits for no one.

So I buried myself in friends and '90s movies and work, trying to act normal. But there was no stopping the way my heart sped up in his presence. It was impossible not to, the way he filled a room. Sarah asked me twice if something was wrong, and I saw that Linda spoke to her once in the break room but fell abruptly silent when I entered.

So I put a pep in my step and smiled broadly at them all every day. I'd be damned if I let him see me upset about the accusations he'd thrown my way. It made it all the more clear —to open yourself up was to allow people to disappoint you. To leave.

And there was no way I was making that mistake again.

21

ADA

When Vivienne called, I didn't feel the slightest hesitation in saying yes for the first time in months. "Of course I want to go out!"

It should have been fun. It had *always* been fun before. Or rather, it had always been necessary before. Numbing, a kind of escape, where I could be no one and someone at the same time. Where I was looked at without being seen.

"Can you believe that Tim would do that? What an *ass*," Vivienne snorted. "It's not like he's even that handsome."

I nodded and took another sip of the martini I'd ordered. Vivienne was probably on her third already—she hadn't noticed that I wasn't keeping up with her, and I was glad for that.

"Anyway, I'm happy you're soon free of that internship, Addie! I'm so excited we can start hanging out again. It's like you basically fell off of the earth."

"Yeah, it was kinda demanding." And all-engrossing. And great.

"Where do you want to go tonight, after this? Benny's is open again, I think, though it's quite far. How about Bumble and Berry? Their new bouncer is delicious. He always lets us skip the line."

"Anywhere is fine with me," I said. "What have you been doing these months?"

"Oh, this and that." She flicked dark hair back. "I was in Tulum for a bit in January. Spent some time up in Maine recently." Her phone buzzed and she looked down immediately. I spun my glass around, awkwardly looking at the people around us. The bar was mostly empty—it was only a hotel bar, after all. Classy jazz played in the background. "Oh, and I'm sort of dating a new guy at the moment," Vivienne added, still looking down at her phone.

"That's great! Who?"

"His name is Ty. He and his friends will join us, and then we all roll out to Bumble and Berry. Oh, Addie, you need another drink!"

She laughed and waved the waiter over. I smiled obligingly and ordered another martini. Why couldn't I get back into the easygoing person I had been?

We made pleasant small talk and I let her dictate the conversation, smiling and laughing at the appropriate times. What had we ever really had in common? I suddenly couldn't remember.

"Here's the man of the hour, finally!" Vivienne gave a squeal and bounced out of her seat, hugging each of the boys in turn.

The first turned to me with a glazed look. "Hello, blondie."

"Hi. I'm Ada. Are you Ty?"

"That's right." He took a seat opposite me, in the seat Viv had just vacated. In one sweep he finished her drink. "So this place seems like kind of a drag."

One after another, the others filed in next to us until I was at the back of the table, people on each side. "It's all right," I said. "Quiet."

"Too quiet. Look at the people here. They all look like they want to shoot themselves," one of the guys said, his hair artfully slicked back, and everyone laughed—Vivienne hardest of all. I looked around. People looked fine, just minding their own business.

"Let's do a round of shots before we head out."

"I don't think this is a shots kind of place…" I began, but Ty had already waved the waitress over. The following exchange was excruciatingly painful to listen to—he was rude in the extreme. She sent me a final, desperate glance.

"Don't worry about it," I said. "Of course we understand."

Two of the guys let out rude snorts and shared looks with one another across the table. The waitress hurried away. I spun my martini around. Months ago, I would probably have found them hilarious. Or I'd be drunk enough that I'd think that I did.

Vivienne slid over to me, moving over Ty's lap to do so. He eyed her appreciatively before reaching across her to me. "Are you going to finish that?"

"No," I said, and slid my drink over to him.

"Hey. Don't look now," Vivienne's breathy voice was in my ear. "But a hot guy at the bar is *totally* checking you out. Like, in an angry, sexy way."

I took another sip of my martini and glanced up slyly at the bar. My heart stopped. Sitting on one of the tall chairs, his long legs stretched out before him and clad in an expensive tailored suit, was Grant.

And he was indeed staring at me.

And he wasn't alone.

Our eyes collided with a force I felt must have been audible—as if we were glued together, as if he was sitting beside me instead of ten feet away. His gaze was heavy with meaning as it broke from mine and flicked over the company around me. It returned to me with a disappointed weight.

How dare he judge me?

Opposite him sat a perky redhead with a notepad and a glass of red wine in front of her. She was glancing down at her phone, but she was very clearly facing him and very clearly primped for a date at a hotel bar. Pumps, a little black dress capped off with three-quarter sleeves. Sensibly dressed. Professional-looking. Probably the type of woman Grant might *actually* see himself with. It felt absurdly as if I was watching him interview a woman for the position of my replacement.

Jealousy and anger burned through me at the sight. My own eyes filled with it, returning to his with all the judgment I could muster. Let him see how angry I could be too.

He broke our gaze and returned it to the short woman next to him. Vivienne leaned in closer. "He looks a bit drab, but hot too, I think. In that quiet way. You should go over there."

"No," I said. "Absolutely not."

The round of shots didn't come, as predicted. The others turned restless real quick.

"Let's go to Bumble and Berry."

"It's not open yet!"

"I know a great place next door," Ty said. "For sure they'll let us in for free, although it might be through the back door."

Coats were tugged on, dollar bills left on the table to cover our martinis. I tried to surreptitiously slip an extra twenty for the waitress, who'd been so poorly treated since the arrival of Viv's friends.

She linked arms with me as we exited the bar, chatting excitedly about the upcoming trip she was taking with her sister's college-aged friends to Cancun. I glanced behind us; Grant was alone now. His date's coat still hung over the chair —had she gone to the bathroom?

"Hey, Viv. I'll meet you guys outside? I'll just be a minute."

She glanced behind me. "Don't tell me you're going to slip him your number while his date is in the ladies'? You're bad, Ada!" She grinned.

"Yes," I agreed wanly and marched over to where he was

sitting. If I gave myself too much time to think about it, I knew I would have chickened out. Action first, thought later. When had that ever gone wrong?

His eyes darkened as he saw me approach.

"Having fun?" he asked, voice silky and distant. I hated when he sounded like that; the old Grant, the superior facade.

"Very." I crossed my arms. "Like you seem to be doing."

He looked over at the mystery woman's coat with a thin veneer of surprise, gone as quickly as it had come. "Ah. That's not what you're imagining, I think."

"I'm sure."

Grant narrowed his eyes. "I thought you were done with your old tricks, Ada. Who were those people?"

I'd been asking myself the same question not ten minutes earlier, but at the judgment in his voice the stubbornness in me reared its ugly head. "They're *great* people. *Just great.* And it's not like who I'm friends with is any of your concern."

He downed the drink he was holding in one quick swallow. "No, that's for damn sure."

"I'm glad to see you're moving on so quickly." I backed away, feeling the acid rise up in my throat. "Hope you manage to give her a good night."

"Likewise," he spat. "Though won't nights spent with that crew jeopardize your little deal with Daddy?"

"You're an ass, you know?"

"See you Monday!"

"Looking forward to it!"

I stormed out of the bar, pulling my coat on tighter as I did. Why did it hurt so bad, talking with him like this? Every part of me felt bruised, even as anger spiraled.

The night air was cool as I emerged from the hotel and my breath rose in little puffs before me, white in the darkness.

Vivienne was leaning against the wall, a cigarette in hand, her long legs crossed. "There you are! Did the flirting go all right?" She wriggled her eyebrows.

"Splendid. Where are the others?"

"They popped to the liquor store around the corner to pick up some more *l'alcool* to down before the bar. I said we'd wait here."

I grabbed her hand in mine. Adrenaline rushed through me, hot and fiery, and I felt jittery from my encounter with Grant.

"Vivienne. I don't want to keep doing this. Going out to these bars all week, hanging around with these types of people. What does Ty do?"

Vivienne looked thunderstruck, blinking at me with heavily mascaraed lashes. "He's one of the new DJs playing at Bumble and Berry. He's going to be someone someday."

"Maybe. Maybe not. But he seems like a genuinely terrible person. Did you hear the way he scolded that poor waitress in there?" I said. "And you deserve someone better. We haven't been very good friends to each other in the past, Viv. You know that. We'd rile each other up and push each other to go further and further on every night out."

"But that was fun." She looked disbelieving. "We were having *fun*, Ada."

I shook my head slowly. "I don't think that was what we were really seeking. Call me when you want to talk about something real, Viv. When you want to meet up in daylight."

"You think you're better than me," she gaped. "Do you want me to remind you of all the shit you pulled last year? Or the year before?"

"I don't need you to," I said, trying to summon my courage to announce the decision I'd already made. "But I'm going to get help. And I wish that you would, too."

She was still watching me when I got into the cab I hailed, staring after me with indecipherable eyes. I prayed she would sort herself out and surround herself with better people. I promised myself that I would contact her again, as soon as I got back to New York. When I could try to have a proper conversation with her.

When I was who I wanted to be again.

Addie.

Both my mother and brother had called me that. Maybe I could find her again, be her again. I knew I owed it to them both to try. And I owed it to myself.

22

GRANT

It had been a couple of days, but I still couldn't believe that she had been out with them again.

It confirmed everything.

I was such a fool to have considered opening myself up to her when she was clearly not discerning with those she spent her time with. Me in the diner by her house one night, ten drunk and high fools who harassed waiters the next.

Maybe she told everyone stories of her grief and childhood. Maybe she had told them to me, sensing that there was something to be gained from that. That I could somehow be worked into sharing more of myself. The damnedest of it all was that it had been *working*.

But that was over now. If there was one thing I'd learned for sure, it was that I had been right about Ada Hathaway from the start—and right in my decision not to let women in. It did you no good.

It had certainly not been a date I'd been on, but an interview with Jenna Marlon of *Art Weekly*. But when Ada had spoken to me like that... well, I hadn't minded if she got the wrong impression. Perhaps that had been silly of me. I shook my head as if to clear the thought away. What was done was done.

The small calendar on my desk had the date 30th of March marked with a small, black x. The day her internship would come to an end. I'd put the mark there nearly a month ago, after the first time in the storage room. The little x stared at me, reminding me of my naivety. At the time I had been looking forward to it.

I still did, but for entirely different reasons. So that she could be out of my life for good, and I could return to my normal habits and my normal work without any blonde, irritatingly witty distractions.

And now it was only three days away. *Three more days.*

I could handle that. I knew I could.

The lawyers rang after lunch.

"Grant Wood."

There was a deep sigh on the other side. "Hi, Grant, it's Roger from Brent and Gail. We have a problem."

Someone, somewhere, was accusing me of embezzling funds from the company. It was ridiculous—*stupid*—and entirely unfounded. And yet the documents they'd sent over for me to peruse made it all very clear. Someone had documents allegedly proving that I had siphoned massive amounts of money from auctions and into my own pockets.

It would be a long, drawn-out legal battle—one I didn't need right now.

Linda popped her head in.

"Can I talk to you for a moment, sir?"

"Yes." I put down the papers the lawyers had emailed me. If this was actually happening, we needed to prepare. I'd call them back later.

She closed the door behind her and sank down into the chair opposite my desk with a wide smile. "It's Ada's last day on Friday."

"Yes, I'm aware."

"I think we should organize a goodbye present, something to show that she's been valued while she's been here."

Damn it. "I'm not against that. Talk to HR and see what you can come up with."

"Will do. It'll be from all of us." Linda rose to leave, pausing by the still-closed door. "They've been through a lot, that family. She deserves to be happy."

I bristled under her gaze. "Yes, she does."

Linda gave a short nod, as if something had been decided, and left my office.

I shook my head in exasperation. Linda was too intuitive for her own good—and my shot at making Ada happy was bound to fail. I ought to have told her that, if it wouldn't have jeopardized everything.

A courier arrived with a bottle of forty-year old Macallan after lunch, wrapped in a beautiful wooden cask. It was delivered and put on my conference table. I sighed and rose, digging through the packaging to fish out the card. Doubtless some client who wanted to impress us, or a competitor who tried to brag with sales numbers. It wouldn't be the first time it had happened.

But no. It was from Arthur.

Thanks for taking Ada on. I owe you one, Grant.

Fucking hell. Had everyone conspired today to remind me Ada was leaving soon?

And he did not owe me. I owed him *everything*. Perhaps I needed to do a better job of conveying that in the future.

23

ADA

The office was eerily quiet when I entered. There was no cheerful hello from Linda, no lopsided smile from Adam. No morning meeting.

"Hello?" I asked. "Where is everyone?"

Sarah came out from the copier room. "Hey, Ada," she said with a taut smile. "Something's happened."

Fear gripped ahold of me. Things were never good when someone started a conversation like that. Had there been an accident? Where was Grant? I couldn't handle it if something had happened.

"Tell me."

"Grant's been charged with embezzlement. He's down talking to the lawyers and the police right now."

"That's ludicrous."

"We think so too." She shook her head. "Linda is down there, pacing outside the interrogation room."

"Has it hit the media yet?"

"No. But it likely will."

Thoughts flicked through my head, moving faster and faster with each step. Grant Wood loved this company. He had made it into what it was today; he lived and breathed it. He had more money than anyone could spend in a lifetime—

there was no need for him to embezzle. Throwing everything he had built away?

"This reeks," I said.

"That's what Adam said too," Sarah said. "He's down with our second team of lawyers, trying to hammer out where the accusations first came from. Whether or not evidence had been forged."

Anger rose up in my chest, hot and furious. "There can only be one person behind this," I said. I fumbled with the clasp to my bag. "I'm going to call Ben Harris, and you're going to record this conversation."

Sarah immediately fished up her phone out of her pocket, voice hard. "Are you certain this is a good idea?"

I hesitated with my finger over the call button. "No," I admitted. "But I'm too angry to do anything else."

He replied on the first ring, smug voice clear.

"Ada! I knew you'd forgotten to thank me for something."

"Trumped up charges? Surely that's low, even by you."

Rich laughter spilled out of the phone. "Now, now, Ada, I don't possibly know what you mean by that."

"Clever, really. How did you get the FBI to give you the time of day?"

"Surprising, really, how accommodating people get with a bit of money."

I bit my lip. "Which department at Jack and Thorn's did you work for again before you took over the operating role? Books and Manuscripts?"

There was a brief, stunned silence on the other end. Then his smug voice returned. "You've been reading about me?"

"I suppose one of your trade skills was to spot a forgery."

"You know, I always suspected you were smarter than you let on. It's a shame you're so devoted to Grant, but I suppose we all have different tastes. Some might prefer cardboard."

"This is too far, even in this ridiculous war of yours."

He laughed. "Nothing personal, of course. I did what I had to."

The line clicked off. Sarah gave a shaky sigh of relief and clicked off the sound of the recording.

"Wow. I can't believe it. He all but admitted it."

"I knew he wouldn't be able to help it. If there's one thing he loves to do, it's gloating."

"Ada, we need to get this to the police. Right away."

"Can we just stop an interrogation like that?"

She bit her lip. "No. But the lawyers should hear it. They'll know what to do."

And they did. Mr. Tyron, the lawyer who had been on the company's retainer for as long as I could remember, shook his head when he heard the recorded phone call.

"The man's an imbecile," he said. "What's in those forged documents is skillful, yes, but might also land him in court for attempted slander and fraud."

"Mr. Harris?"

"Yes. That was a huge risk he took."

"I don't think he ever suspected it might lead back to him."

"And clearly he didn't think you clever enough to consider using a basic recording device," Adam muttered next to us. "Can we get Grant released immediately with this?"

"It'll take a couple of days. The accusations are serious, and I think it would be better for the legitimacy of the company and for the investigation if Grant sat out from the office for a few days. Let him work from home. His next in command can be acting CEO—that would be you, Adam?"

"Yes. Grant won't like that, however."

Mr. Tyron sighed. "He sure won't. But Mr. Wood doesn't have a choice in this particular matter. For the board to remain confident in his leadership I would say it's a necessity."

"How long until his name can be entirely cleared?"

"Depends on how long until we can prove definitively that there is considerable and plausible doubt that these documents are real. Shouldn't take long, with this." He gave the phone a small wave. "Now we know where to start looking."

The office was a strange mixture of mayhem and calm after that. Grant was sent to collect his coat from the upstairs office and was then swiftly escorted out of the building. He looked tall and annoyed, but I thought that his jaw was clenched tight. To go through that and know you were innocent... having to leave your own company because of unfounded accusations. It was what Ben had wanted, and it annoyed me to no end that he had managed to succeed—for a few days, at the very least.

"Listen up, everyone," Adam said with crossed arms. "We are going to keep this ship afloat until Grant returns. This is nothing new—we do as we've always done. Auctions continue. Marketing continues. Customer service most definitely continues to be excellent." He straightened his glasses and gave a slight, nervous cough. "And if you have any questions or concerns, you're welcome to direct them to me or Sarah."

A few days without the ability to come into the office—if there was anything that threatened to kill him, it might be that. Grant lived and breathed this job.

It was a testament to how well he'd drilled this office that few things changed in Grant's absence. Adam directed us all efficiently, ensuring that all t's were crossed and i's dotted while carrying out his normal duties.

"Gosh," I once heard him mutter to himself as he sat in front of his computer. "He needs to stop emailing us so damn much."

I tried and failed to stop the smile spreading across my face. That sounded exactly like the insufferable, difficult-to-like Grant I knew.

The Grant who still hadn't apologized for accusing me of seducing him with the sole purpose of gaining access to my trust fund.

And so the days continued, despite all the craziness and lawyers and questions.

Minna: I've just heard about the boss man. It hit the newspapers today.

Ada: Don't remind me. I'm helping our public relations team do damage control now.

Minna: Is it true?

Ada: Absolutely not.

Minna: I guess you're not seeing much of him now then?

I looked up at his office, the lights still out. No one had been in there apart from the cleaners since he'd been forced out of the office, a tall and lean figure emanating annoyance.

Ada: Not at all. If I'm lucky, I might even finish my internship without seeing him.

Minna: Are you still intent on going?

I smiled and sent a screenshot of the plane tickets I'd booked just that morning, my heart in my throat. The nerves lessened as soon as the purchase went through, when the decision was made, even if I still found it hard to believe that I'd actually committed to this.

Ada: 100% I am.

Minna: Are you really, truly sure that you're okay with not seeing him before you leave? I mean, I'm all for it, but just in case.

I sighed. Typical Minna to not let you get away with anything, having to pry. Not that it wasn't good for me—it just forced me to be a tad more introspective than was my custom.

Ada: Yes. He accused me of something vile, made light of everything that happened between us, and then went out on a date with someone else. I'm done, Minna. It's not worth the pain.

Minna: I'm proud of you.

I smiled and sent her a heart-eyed emoji. Sometimes it wasn't so bad to have a friend who studied psychology and regularly used you as a test subject.

And the thing was—he didn't return. The days passed quickly.

"Dear," Linda said after lunch before my final day, "will you be so kind and drop some documents off to Grant on your way home from work? I know you live close by."

"I thought he handled most things via email? That's how all of us have been handling documents these days."

"I know, honey, but these are confidential and need to be signed in person." She handed me a stack of thick manila folders. "He'll know what it's about."

They felt heavy in my hands, dread in my stomach. So much for being able to avoid him before I left.

But maybe I could make it into something positive. Clear the air between us, leave with no regrets and nothing unsaid. After all the recent talk with Minna, closure was on my mind. And in the newfound spirit of not running away or shying from the ugly... I'd deliver them to him.

Tomorrow I'd work my last day.

And the day after, I'd leave New York behind.

24

ADA

I heard the doorbell ring on the other side. My heart beat so loudly I could hear it, audibly, as I waited for him to open the door. *Hello. Here are your documents. Thanks for these months. Also, you're an ass. Bye. See you never.*

Perfect. Adult, classy, and just a bit petulant.

I shook my head and tried to get my emotions under control as footsteps approached on the other side. The door swung open.

"Hello." Grant's expression registered surprise but swiftly shifted into something guarded. His shirt was rolled up to his elbows, lazily tucked into a pair of gray suit pants. He was too attractive for his own good.

"Linda sent me over with documents for you to sign." I held them up in front of me as if they were a shield.

"Great. Come in."

The dining-room table had been transformed into a copy of his office, an open laptop humming and papers strewn about. A large cup of coffee sat atop a stack of books.

"You're bugging everyone in the office with all your emails, you know," I pointed out.

He looked up from the documents I'd brought. "Huh? Yeah. But they need to know what to do."

"We do," I said. "Both you and Adam are making sure of that."

"Have you heard that Ben Harris has been caught on tape confessing to setting me up?" He snorted. "I always knew he was too pompous for his own good. It'll only be a matter of time until the lawyers can get the whole thing dismissed. And then we'll sue him for slander."

"Yeah, I heard something about that." I wrapped my arms around myself. His hair was disheveled, and the stupid urge to run my fingers through it and see the frown on his face relax returned.

He paused at the table. "I understood that no one in the executive branch believed the rumors."

"Of course not."

"Thank you for trusting me, Ada."

"Everyone at the firm did. The idea that you'd embezzle is absurd."

There was the faint sound of his fingers tapping against the table. "I'll admit that it came as a surprise."

He'd worked for this company for *seven years*. I'd seen employees linger around corners to try to time when he arrived at work, just so they could later claim they'd said hi to the maverick boss who singlehandedly brought Hathaway's into the 21st century. *And he thought no one cared?* Sadness and anger chased one other inside me.

"It's nice to be believed," I said softly. "When you're deserving of it."

"About that…. I'm sorry, Ada. I've thought a lot about what happened the night after Harry's retirement party. I was wrong."

"You were," I said, wrapping my arms tighter around myself as if I could somehow smother the emotions rising up inside. This would not do. I was leaving in two days, damn it.

"And I have to admit that you've done a good job at Hathaway's, regardless of what your initial motivation was."

My heart beat with an aching, staccato rhythm. *Damn* him

for doing this now. I'd made the decision not to let him in. It hurt too much when he'd leave again, retreat back into his shell. There was no way I could handle that again.

"And you've turned out to be a fairly decent boss, despite what I initially feared."

His lip curled slightly at that. "Tomorrow's your last day. Are the others taking you out?"

"No," I said. "I didn't want to."

"Got plans with your friends?" He looked back down at the table, his tone turning dismissive.

"No. And the people you saw me with aren't actually my friends."

"I thought they were great people?"

"Not really. They are people I used to spend time with once. I thought I'd give it another try, for old time's sake, but…" I shrugged.

Grant's gaze caught mine, face still impassive but eyes intense. "Glad to hear it. You deserve better."

My mouth went dry. Why did he say things like this? He was the one who had gone on a date not *a week* after we'd argued.

"I might say the same about you," I said coolly. "The woman you were out with looked like a stock photo, Grant." I said it as an insult, sneering, tapping into the teen I'd once pretended to be on occasion. Only then did it strike me that it might be exactly what Grant would want in a woman—stiff, beautiful perfection, all trim edges and neat seams.

He gave a humorless laugh. "It was an interview with a reporter. Not a date."

I bit my lip. His eyes were locked on mine as if daring me to object. It made sense, even if it was an odd place to choose to conduct such a meeting.

"Doesn't change anything," I murmured. "I was never using you. Can you believe that? Not just think it—actually believe it, Grant."

He rose abruptly and moved to the window. His hands

were in his pockets, and it looked like they were knotted so tightly that his knuckles must have been white. For a long moment, I didn't think he would answer.

"I don't do relationships, Ada. I can't."

A hard knot settled in my stomach. "What you're saying is that you don't *want* to try to have something real."

Grant shook his head. "It's not giving up when there's no chance at all. It was a bad idea for us both to get involved. Come on, you knew that from the start, too."

"I did," I said. "I guess somewhere along the line I just decided you were worth it."

I saw his shoulders tremble slightly at that. Anger rose up in me. He'd accused me of faking everything with him, potentially dated someone else, and then he had the audacity to say we'd been doomed from the start. Like that was the reason what we had couldn't continue.

"But these are all flimsy excuses. I think you're scared. And do you know why I think that? Because I am too. What I feel for you terrifies me. It *terrifies* me, Grant. And yet I tried, and I'm saying it now, because I want to be honest with you about that. And you have the nerve to shut me out?"

Grant shook his head. "No, Ada, it's not that simple."

"Of course it is. It's only complicated if you make it." I stifled the sob rising up in my chest. "It's either that, or you don't care about me at all. I can handle both. But don't try to lie to me."

"There is no future for us."

I nodded and looked back down at the papers on his desk. They were far easier to face than his gaze. "Can you sign the documents now please, so I can take them to the office tomorrow?"

He bent and finished off each page, writing his name in bold, sharp strokes of black ink. There was a jerkiness to his movements I wasn't used to seeing, none of his normal grace or self-composure.

184

"Ada," he murmured when the last one was finished. "I never meant to hurt you."

"Well, you did." I took the stack of papers from him and slid them back into the manila envelope. "Goodbye, Grant. I'm sure you'll be back as acting CEO in no time—the lawyers say it's just a formality now."

I moved to leave, swinging my bag across my shoulder.

"Congratulations on your last day," he said abruptly. "I'll be happy to write you a recommendation letter if you want. For whatever you're heading off to do next."

I couldn't help it—I laughed. Of course that would be what he said now. I moved to the door. "Great. I appreciate that."

"Friends, Ada?"

I turned back, a sad smile on my face. "Were we ever, really?"

The door closed behind me with finality.

———

There is no future for us.

Which, of course, was code for *I don't want you in my future.*

The words hurt because of the truth in them. He wasn't an impulsive person; he was someone who planned and plotted his life. And if he genuinely couldn't see a way to work me into it, it was because he didn't want me there. And that hurt more than I had ever expected it to.

Well, that was that. At least we'd had it out one last time. I'd tried, and been burned, and now we could both move on. I knew I didn't need any more distractions. Where I was heading tomorrow would be challenging enough.

Sarah dropped a small, silvery bag on my desk after lunch, an expectant smile on her face.

"Go on," she said. "Open it."

Adam peered around the corner, and I saw Linda smiling

from her desk. "It's from all of us. A little farewell present," she called.

"You guys. You shouldn't have!"

"We had to. You're the best executive intern we've ever had!"

I gave Sarah a measured look. "I'm also the first."

"Yes, well, that doesn't matter. Come on, look inside."

I laughed and opened the bag. Inside lay a small silver box wrapped with gold ribbon and a packet of chocolate truffles. I fished out the silver box and opened it carefully. Inside lay a small replica of the statue of Artemis from Burch's collection, the one we successfully sold to a museum in Milan.

"The crowning achievement of your internship," Adam said.

"Thank you. It's been a pleasure working with all of you," I said, mortified to feel tears threatening to well up. "It's been one of the best experiences of my life."

"The same for us, dear," Linda said softly. "It's just a shame the CEO himself can't be here and see you off."

I looked down at the small silver box. "Yes. Such a shame."

The receptionist gave me a wide smile when I turned in my security card and password generator at the end of the day. The sun was still out for another hour, and the frosty spring air had started to give way to the warmth of approaching summer.

"Thanks for this time, Miss Hathaway," she told me. "Have a good one."

"You too, Darlene. You too."

At home, my bag was already packed by virtue of my sleepless nights. The place felt empty, this little apartment that Dad had bought for me directly after graduation. A place neither my mother nor Max had ever been in, a place only for me and mine. That had saddened me for so long. But maybe I could make it into a proper home when I returned.

I wiped down all the surfaces, pulled out electric appliances from the outlets, made sure there was no perishable food in the fridge. The car would be downstairs soon to drive me to JFK. Outside my living-room windows, the skyline of New York glittered on, as endless and beautiful as a night sky.

"See you later," I whispered.

25

GRANT

The lawyers managed to get the case dismissed in record time, allowing me to return to the firm the following week. After board meetings and talking with the staff, it became clear that no one had believed in the embezzlement rumors.

"They were like a smoke screen," one of the board members told me. "We are all aware of the feud with Jack and Thorn's. It was always clear they were involved, one way or another."

Arthur had been outraged, calling me daily in an unusual outpouring of support. Not one board member had put forth a motion to dismiss me from my position as a CEO. As far as I could tell, it hadn't even been discussed.

And they were just as hungry for revenge as I was.

"How likely do you think it'll be to get him with the tape?" I asked Roger.

"I'd say it's 50-50. It didn't take a lot of digging to discover the accusations were false, so I believe it was rather an attempt to bury us in paperwork and litigation. It would put you out of the office, sir, and our stockholders in a tizzy."

"And in the meanwhile, they could keep poaching our clients."

He nodded. "While we'd like to use the tape to prove

slander and fraudulent behavior, the way it was obtained means it would be inadmissible in court."

"That's a shame. I never heard the story of how, exactly, you got it?"

Roger smiled. "The youngest Hathaway. Why, she called him, suspecting that he wouldn't be able to resist bragging, and she made sure a colleague taped the whole conversation."

"Ada? She was the one who gave you the tape?"

"Yes. Not a day after the accusation against you was first made."

My hands tightened along the edge of my desk. I'd assumed it had been leaked from within his own firm. How had she managed that? She must have tricked Ben, figured out immediately that he was behind this.

Hell, she had gotten to that conclusion faster than the lawyers.

"Can I hear it? The tape?"

"Yes. I'll leave a copy of it behind here. But just to remind you—this cannot leave the ongoing investigation."

"It won't."

He stood to leave, putting a silver USB on the desk. "I'll keep you updated."

I spun the USB around in my hand, thinking. "Hey. We might not be able to use this in a court. But how about we make sure that the board of Jack and Thorn's gets it?"

Roger smiled. "They would fire him as CEO. Fraud is not something they could ever condone."

"Exactly. Say what you will about Ben Harris, but his firm is not entirely rotten."

"We'll have it done tomorrow, sir."

I leaned back and watched him go, the USB a small but palpable weight in my hand. Ada had made the call, had made sure we got the proof needed to clear my name.

I plugged it into the computer and hit play. Even through the poor quality of the recording, the anger in Ada's voice was palpable. She'd called to defend me—furious even before she got his admission.

She'd never once believed I was guilty.

And I had believed she was playing me right away, as soon as her father told me about the trust fund. I leaned forward and put my head in my hands. I had managed to push her away, and somehow she had retained her belief in me. Not her respect, though—that much had been clear after she dropped by my house. How did anyone try to be good enough to live up to that?

She was a genuinely good person, through and through, kind in ways I'd rarely encountered before. Sharp as a blade.

There was no way I could hear this tape and not make sure that she knew I was aware of her help.

I stopped at her building after work to thank her.

"Mr. Wood." Billy greeted me with a grin. "Come to visit Miss Hathaway?"

"Yes. Could you call up, please?"

"I'm afraid she's not in, sir."

"All right. I'll just leave a message with reception for when she's back."

"Certainly. But between you and me, sir, that might take a while. She left last weekend with some real luggage."

"Left? As in, for traveling?"

"That's Miss Hathaway's personal business, sir. All I'm saying is that perhaps calling might be the faster option, if you've got something urgent to convey."

"Okay. Well, thank you."

She'd left? Immediately after finishing her internship?

Maybe she left because of me, because of the argument and the things I'd said. *We have no future.* It was still true. I knew I'd disappoint her. Hell, I already had, and we weren't even in a relationship.

But I knew I was being self-centered. She'd probably left with friends, finally free of the internship. Eager to get away.

Even so, she needed to know that I was grateful, that I

knew I had her to thank for getting the embezzlement charges dropped and my name cleared. Without her quick thinking... the board might have swung in an entirely different direction.

I owed her everything.

Her name on my phone shone with bright, abrasive light. I typed a quick thank-you, careful to keep it professional.

Grant: I heard you were the one who made sure we got Ben Harris's confession on tape. Smart thinking. Thank you, Ada.

The answer was immediate.

Ada: No worries. Knew you weren't an embezzler.

And that was that. I slid the phone into the running pocket of my track pants and headed out, back into the darkness of Central Park and the steady oblivion of burning lungs and aching legs. No need to think about where she was, what she was doing. With whom.

She was gone. I would be more productive. The sun still shone.

Everything was great.

Except, of course, that it wasn't.

It's an odd thing, when a storm has passed, leaving the weather once again calm. But it's wrecked everything in its path. Moved things around, rearranged trees and rocks and fences until the landscape is the same but the features forever altered.

I didn't know how to adapt in the world she'd left behind.

Linda made veiled hints about Ada being in Europe for the spring, disappearing just after the internship ended. It had been nearly two weeks and no one had heard from her in the office. It was as if she had disappeared, fallen off the earth, returned to where she had come from.

Was she with that group of people I'd seen her with at the hotel? She'd denied they were friends, but if she was with them, I couldn't imagine them being up to anything good.

There was one easy answer. Arthur.

But I wouldn't sink that low just to sate my stupid curiosity.

No, I did something far worse—I downloaded social media apps with the express purpose of looking her up. I was painfully thankful that she didn't have her Instagram profile set to private so I could lurk in blissful anonymity.

But there were no new posts. The last had been from the Charity Auction ball, a photo of her and Sarah posing in front of the company's logo. Clad in an achingly familiar shimmery dress, she stared at me from the screen, a genuine smile on her face. *One of the perks of my job is getting to work together with this one,* she had captioned it. Sarah had commented with two little heart-eyed emojis. There were no other photos of Hathaway's and nothing since.

Why hadn't she posted in over two months? Before there had been frequent updates, on and off, pictures of clubs and the park and one over the bleak Hudson River where the caption read *I wish I could paint again.* There were no comments. Had she painted once?

Why didn't I know that?

I groaned. It had been weeks. I needed to move on—preferably yesterday. But the only thing I saw when I closed my eyes was her dancing eyes, teasing me and telling me to stop being so serious. Being with her had been like breathing, and now that she'd left, I felt as if I hadn't drawn a proper breath in days.

A tentative knock sounded at the door. "Mr. Wood?"

"Come in."

A timid face poked in. Rob, the new intern. Linda had enjoyed having an intern so much that she declared the executive wing should always have one. I humored her for a trial period—if only because I knew she was nearing retirement. I didn't think Rob would last.

"Yes?"

"I read something in a newspaper today that I think you should take a look at. I know you're concerned with the brand." He walked quickly across the room and handed me a newspaper, carefully folded back to reveal one page. I took one look at it.

"Why did you think this was something I'd be interested in?"

"I mentioned it to Linda," he stammered. "She said I should give it to you. That it was a good idea."

I returned my gaze to the sunny blonde staring back at me. It was late April on the French Rivera, and she was already a bit tan. I put it down on my desk as if burned.

"In the future, bring this sort of thing to marketing."

"Yes, sir." He hurried out and shut the door briskly. I ran a hand through my hair, thinking about Ada's admonishments. *You can be too intimidating to people. Not everyone handles criticism like you.* I sighed. I'd have to make it up to him later. It wasn't *technically* his fault that he wasn't a bouncy beauty with a rapier-sharp wit.

Hathaway heiress in St. Tropez, the headline stated. A blurry photograph was shown, unmistakably Ada, in a summer dress. Her hair was curly and natural, and she was talking to a young man in a tux. A waiter, perhaps? I hoped.

The photo was clearly taken at a distance by paparazzi or by some Manhattanite who had recognized her from her earlier stints in the local tabloids.

She looked radiant. I swallowed and put the newspaper away. So she had jetted off to the south of France. Not that I could blame her, really. Why would she stay? She had nothing to stay for. I had made sure of that.

But there was so much more to her than partying. I had thought that that part of her life was over. The woman I had seen, when she had been with me, was someone so radically different than the one I'd witnessed at the hotel bar. The one Arthur had once been so concerned about.

And she had been stellar as an intern. Why wasn't she working? Had I had something to do with that? I couldn't bear it if I had.

The thought gnawed at me for days. Mistakes had been made, most of them mine. But there was no reason I couldn't seek to rectify them somehow.

So I sank lower.

"Grant?"

"Hey, Arthur. Am I bothering you?"

"No, not at all. I always have time for you." There was the faint sound of waves behind him.

"Are you in the marina?"

"Yeah, just put the boat in." He cleared his throat. "What do you need?"

Ah. I had understood early on that the sailing boat had been something he shared with Max and Ada, and then increasingly only Max, who had taken up the sport with vigor. I *had* called at a bad time.

"Do you know where Ada is? I've understood she's out of the country."

"Of course. Why do you ask?"

I sighed. "Some of us at the office were curious, and wondering when she would be likely to return. Together with HR, I was thinking of offering her a more permanent position in the company, should she want it."

There was a stunned silence. "Truly?"

"Yes. She has the education and drive for it, and we're all very pleased with her performance."

"I think she'd be interested in that. Of course."

"Do you know when she will be back?"

"No. There is no set timeline. I have to be honest with you, Grant, but she's at a retreat in the south of France."

"At a retreat." There were only two sorts of places people like Arthur Hathaway might call a "retreat." The first was a spa, and the second a rehab center. My stomach clenched in fear at the thought of it being the second. What had happened?

"Yes. It's run by a therapist she found. Has some really legitimate points, actually. Anyhow, Ada is working through some stuff now. And as much as I think she would be interested in the job offer, I know she's set on finishing what she's doing before she returns."

I was briefly stunned into silence. "Yes. Yes, of course. I'll make sure to have the conversation with her when she returns."

"But I know she'd love it if you gave her a call."

"She would?"

"Yes. I know you two are friends now. She's not locked away, Grant," he said with a laugh. "I talk to her every day."

Every day. *Every day?* When had that ever been the case? They hadn't been close.

"All right. Thanks for the info, Arthur."

"Sure thing. See you around, Grant."

"Bye."

So she wasn't jet-setting around in the countryside. She was working through her grief and had chosen to get licensed help in doing so. I'd always known Ada was clever, but now I saw just how brave she was, too. She'd faced her demons.

Perhaps I could, too.

My concierge had a package for me that night, a solid weight wrapped in purple and pink gift paper. A small bright note was attached to it.

"This was delivered to me?"

"Yes."

"Are you sure?"

Rodman, the concierge in his late sixties who ruled my apartment building like his own kingdom, drew himself up to his full height. "Yes, sir. I am certain."

"Thanks." I ripped off the card and read it, waiting for the elevator to arrive.

For Grant Wood.
I hope this will help you.
Life's too short for fear.
- The friend of a friend.

The i's were dotted with hearts.

I turned back to the reception, ignoring the open elevator.

"Rodman, did you see who left this? Were you here?"

"Yes. I never leave my post."

"What did she look like?"

He considered. "Brown-haired, young. One of your admirers, I'm sure, sir."

"Okay. All right. Thank you."

"Anytime."

I returned to the elevator with that description and his odd inflection on *admirers*. As soon as the doors closed and I was out of his view I ripped into the gift paper.

A brand-new copy of How to Act with Love.

The subtitle read: The key to building loving, lasting relationships.

I stared, and then I broke out into laughter, so loud that it echoed off the steel walls of the elevator.

26

ADA

I painted. I laughed. I visited every damn museum in Provence.

But more than that, I talked and cried and shouted inside of Dr. Willis's office. There was never a set topic, and whatever I wanted to explore was allowed. It had been disconcerting, our first session.

"I understood from your email that you haven't been to a therapist for a couple of years."

"That's right. I have a lot of things bottled up," I said. "I think it's going to take time, and I think there's a very good chance that I'm going to want to stop at some point. But if I don't process the past, I don't think I'm going to be able to have a happy future."

"Good. Anything that's easy isn't worth doing." She had leaned back in her office chair and looked at me with intelligent, appraising eyes. "If you're willing to work then so am I."

And work we did.

She was a caring, no-nonsense kind of therapist. There were always questions, proddings, ways of looking at things that I hadn't tried before.

The nights when I cried returned again, but there was no

corner shop and no late-night calls from Viv. And when I woke up, I felt lighter. It took time, but it worked, all this talking and diving into and sorting through my past. Finding ways of approaching issues actively, and not just from a defensive or reactionary viewpoint. It was on her recommendation that I began checking in with my dad every day. Pushing through the awkwardness, we found a new routine.

"Hey Ada," he'd say. "What have you been up to today?"

As if I was still twelve and coming home from school. But I told him, and asked him in return, listening to him recount the few things he actually did in the Hamptons. For the first time, I realized just how lonely he was.

"He's grieving too," Dr. Willis said one day. "And it takes work to see beyond that." And like that, with daily ten-minute phone calls, we got used to one another again.

Minna didn't stay away, either. She'd taken to an odd hero-worship of Dr. Willis, evident in most of our text conversations.

Minna: When I come to visit, can I meet her?

Ada: Sure. I can probably bring you along for a session.

Minna: OMG! I would love that.

Ada: And then you HAVE to come with me to this amazing little museum I found.

Minna: That's all you want to talk about. Art, art, art.

Ada: No. I also talk about art.

Minna: Funny. Hey, I've been wanting to show you something that I saw today. I'm not sure how you'll take it, but I think you should read it.

She sent me photos of a four-page spread of *Art Weekly*.

The elusive genius of Grant Wood, the title read. Re-introducing Hathaway's.

A beautiful, glossy image of Grant leaning against the goods down in the vaults—in the tomb, to be precise. The vaulted ceiling stretched on behind him, treasures of all kinds mingled in the background. A dusty Ming vase stood on a crate beside him. Grant was clad in a tailored suit, hands in pockets, and looked at the camera without smiling. Everything about the image radiated power, and control, and a touch of the whimsical—just like we'd once said.

I smiled, seeing it. He looked as if he was counting the seconds until this was done. I could imagine him having told the photographer to hurry up just before this photo was taken. There was no way the magazine could have known about the tomb. Grant must have suggested it. Warmth spread through my chest.

But I stopped at the first sentence.

"I'm seated at the W hotel bar, waiting for the elusive Grant Wood of Hathaway's. Since becoming CEO four years ago, he has notoriously not given a single public interview, preferring instead to let the auctions and sales numbers talk. And talk they have."

So she *had* been a reporter. I remembered the notepad and groaned, hurrying to read through the article. His responses were articulate, short, with the right amount of humor and self-awareness. This was a great piece. I could imagine Marc squealing as he read it.

There were even questions about his background, his childhood. My hands shook as I read it. How had he allowed this?

"Did you come from a background of art and culture?"

"No. It was something that struck me in my late teens."

The two final questions stalled me, and I had to sit down, zooming in on the phone to absorb every last word.

"You took over after Arthur Hathaway himself, becoming the first CEO not of the old Hathaway branch. Was that daunting to you?"

"No. Arthur has been a great mentor, and I have nothing but the utmost respect for him. So when he offered me the reins, and the board agreed, I had complete confidence in their choice."

"There's talk that Ada Hathaway, the youngest Hathaway, recently interned at your office. Did she live up to the family name?"

"It's true that she was accepted to an executive intern position.

Ada has a degree in art history and is an incredibly hard worker, shows initiative and discipline. She is a credit both to herself and to the company."

Me? He'd been asked about me?

And he'd sung my praises. Even when he thought I had been using him, doing all of it for my trust fund, he'd said this. He had to have known it would be published and spread amongst all those in the art world in New York, not to mention the entire country.

He'd basically given them all my CV.

It was stupid for this to mean anything, but combined with the text message he'd sent me... I knew that he cared. I could *feel* that he cared, had seen it in his eyes the last time we'd spoken.

It was a shame he hadn't been able to act on it. I made a note to ask Dr. Willis about that the next time our conversations drifted to him, as they had done tentatively in the past.

Sometimes you had to hurt in order to heal. It would undoubtedly be painful.

But I had stopped being afraid of pain.

It was nearly midnight a week later when my phone rang. I put down the book I was reading and dragged myself out of bed. Those who called me regularly all knew I was here— they adjusted to the time difference. If this was a salesman I'd have some *strong* words ready for them.

But the name flashing across my screen made me pause. It was with shaking hands that I pressed answer.

"Grant?"

"Hi, Ada. I'm sorry to bother you."

"No. You're not."

"In the spirit of our old midnight phone calls, I tried to time it when it was midnight in France."

"What time is it for you?"

"Six in the afternoon." He cleared his throat. "I'm walking home from work."

A silence stretched out between us, not awkward, but not particularly comfortable either.

"I called—"

"I read—"

"Go ahead."

"Okay. Well, I read the article about Hathaway's in *Art Weekly*."

"You did?"

"Yes. It was good."

"I made sure they took the promotional photos in the storage room, particularly the tomb," he said. "You were right when you said it was the beating heart of the company."

And the first place we'd kissed. Not that I would say that, but I felt as if it hung in the silence between us. My heart was beating fast, adrenaline working its way through my body. I hated that his voice affected me like this, that I hung on to every word. I also loved that he'd called.

"They looked good."

"Thanks." He cleared his throat again and I heard the sound of a car horn.

"Sounds like New York."

"Same old. I was unsure if you would answer if I called, Ada."

"Oh?"

"Yes. Because I made a lot of mistakes. But I wanted to make sure you were all right."

"I'm all right," I whispered. "I'm actually great."

"You are?"

"Yes. I'm in Provence, in this little town. Time moves so slowly here. Too slowly, at first. But now I'm learning to enjoy it."

"I'm glad," he said, and his voice sounded like he was smiling.

"How are you?"

"Oh, you know. The same."

"So still miserable on the inside but stoic on the outside?"

He barked out a laugh. "You never let me off the hook."

"No. I never did."

"Well. I didn't mean to keep you up."

"No worries. Are you almost home?"

"Yes," he said. "Passing by your front door now, actually."

"Wave to Billy for me."

"Will not."

I laughed, softly, into the phone. I felt as if he was just there, within reach, and not a thousand miles and one *we don't have a future* away.

"Thanks for the call."

"Sure. Sleep well."

"You too."

"I will. In a couple of hours."

"Bye, Grant."

"Bye, Ada."

It took me a long time to fall asleep that night, but it wasn't from crying.

27

GRANT

The phone call played through my mind every step of the coming days. Despite my fear, she'd picked up. There hadn't been anger in her voice, only hesitance and caution. I knew I had so much to ask forgiveness for, and talking to her had made it so clear. You only get one shot at life. And I'd be damned if I didn't give Ada my all, even if I was a broken, undeserving mess. If she still wanted me I could man up and rise to the challenge.

But some conversations you just don't have over the phone—and some things are too important to be left to chance. So I called Adam into my office.

"You're doing what?" he'd asked, eyes bugging.

"I'm going on a vacation."

"Now?"

"Yes. Now. It's important, and I'll be gone for a few days. But I trust you can manage everything."

"Will you be available on the phone?"

I considered that. "Maybe, a bit. But don't rely on it."

"All right. Okay. Well…"

"I leave tomorrow morning. I'll prepare briefs for you for what I have in the works the coming days."

"Sure. Great, sir. Um, so where are you going?"

"France."

———

The plane ride was excruciating.

Every possible scenario played out in my head, and my mind spun around, trying to come up with possible solutions. Ways to approach this problem—the right words to use.

Except, that was not the way it had been with Ada. It had been messy, right from the beginning. Perhaps that was what had made it so right.

The book I'd been sent was lying in my lap. I had read it cover to cover twice. At first, it had been with a disdainful air. There had been no question about it in my mind; it would be nonsense. The writings of someone solely looking to sell copies and make disillusioned Millennials feel better about themselves. An emotional get-rich-quick scheme.

Until I'd read a couple of chapters in, and it... stopped being a joke. Words started to make sense. There was a part or two when I had sat at home, feeling that sense of *aha*, like I suddenly understood parts of myself.

But more than anything, the book made it clear to me that you had to reach out and take what you wanted. The world would never give you anything. I had always—always—known this, and yet somehow I had forgotten it entirely with Ada.

Because I wanted her in my life. I knew that now, having tried to live without her. I wanted to try, to invest in a relationship with her. But more than that, I feared that I might never know happiness without her filling my days. If there was one thing I'd realized these lonely weeks, it was that I was head-over-heels in love with her.

And that was *terrifying*.

I'd always thought that whatever powerful men cared for was a fault, a weakness. Something that was often used against them in one way or another—by the media, by their rivals, by their loved ones themselves if a relationship went sour. I'd vowed never to make the same mistake, to never let myself care for another person like that.

But looking out over the glittering Mediterranean Sea as we began our descent, with Ada somewhere below, I realized that wasn't a conscious decision at all. And that once you'd found that person you cared for, you made damn sure you never let go.

———

The drive from the airport in Marseille to the small town of Luberon only took an hour. I'd found a clinic there run by an American therapist whose website showcased olive groves, art classes and winding French cobblestoned streets.

A place to reflect and grow, the website had said. One Dr. Lydia Willis was the head therapist, and they only accepted ten people at a time. It was my best bet.

I had a feeling I might be turned away at the door, but I had to try.

The cab pulled up at the large French mansion, gravel under the tires. The sun shone—I'd flown from a slightly humid spring day in New York to arrive to the warm heat of southern France. It was May, and it showed.

"*Merci,*" I told the driver and handed him a hundred-euro bill. He had instructions to park down the street with my luggage and return when I called. I had no idea how I'd be received, or how long I could stay.

A tall woman with hair pulled back opened the door when I rang. She wore an apron over her dress and had gray in her hair.

"*Bonjour! Qui êtes-vous?*"

"*Bonjour, madame.* My name is Grant. I'm afraid I don't know much more French than that."

"Well then," she replied in perfect English. "I'm Dr. Willis. I run this establishment. Grant, you said?"

"Yes. Grant Wood."

"Good. I've been wondering if you'd show up."

I blinked at her. "Sorry?"

"You're here to visit Ada?"

"Yes. If she wants to see me."

"I think she will." Dr. Willis smiled. "But if she tells you to go, you go, okay? No badgering my patients."

"Of course. I'd never—"

"She's out back. You'll find her in the gardens."

"All right. Thank you."

She shook her head in an exasperated way and pointed to the gravel path that snaked around the building. It was half overgrown with lavender and shrubbery, high spring flowers winding their way through the green. Somewhere, a bird sang, high and clear. Shrugging out of my suit jacket, I rolled up my sleeves. It was a beautiful day.

I could see why Ada had chosen this place.

I've been wondering if you'd show up.

Had they been discussing me, then? Hope unfurled in my chest. The garden was a mix of greenery and flowers, and in the very far end stood Ada.

She was wearing a white linen dress and was laughing as she spoke on her phone, a flush to her cheeks. I stopped dead, watching her from a distance. The strength of her absence hit me like a blow; I had missed her far more than I had let myself admit.

She laughed again and spoke, too far away to hear what she said. With a small smile, she clicked off the call.

I walked forward.

"Hello, beautiful."

She looked up, shock registering across her features. "Grant?"

"Yes."

"You're here," she repeated.

"Yes," I said. "I wanted to see you."

She looked around as if making sure she was still in

Provence, in this little town, and then back at me. Her eyes moved across my face, my shirt, my body.

"Do you want to sit?" she said finally, gesturing to the bench next to her.

"Yes, I do."

We took a seat next to each other, far enough apart that there was no part of us touching. The longing to hug her was so powerful I had to knot my fingers together in my lap to keep from reaching for her.

"You look good," I said, and meant it. The spring sun had given her freckles and a tan complexion, her hair naturally curly and long down her back. I wanted to touch her so badly I had to knot my hands together; I wanted to pull her against me until I felt her lips at the hollow of my throat.

"Thanks." Ada bit her lip. "Grant, why are you here? Is everything okay?"

The spring air was lovely but felt suddenly altogether too warm. I tugged at the collar of my shirt. "I read about you in a magazine. None of us knew where you were, but there was a photo in one of them. Of you in St. Tropez."

"Oh. Some tourist must have snapped a photo," she sighed.

"For a second, I thought you were here to party."

She sighed again. "I was in Antibes over the day to see the Picasso museum. We stopped in St. Tropez for lunch."

"I don't doubt you—I didn't then, either. It was the first thought that crossed my mind, but the Ada I had grown to know wouldn't be here for that. But my curiosity wouldn't die. I needed to know what you were up to, to follow along on your adventures from the sidelines. Your dad said you were here. He didn't want to rat you out, but I called to tell him I wanted to offer you a permanent position in the firm."

"You did?"

"Yes. Because I know you deserve it, and you'd do a great job. And so he told me how to find you."

"Grant, I—"

I cut her off, whatever refusal she had planned. "I was an idiot. In so many ways, Ada. I have... oh, I have made so many mistakes since the first moment you started working at Hathaway's." Her lips opened slightly, startled. "And more than anything, not a day has gone past since we parted where I haven't thought about you."

Her mouth dropped open slightly, but there was no response. I reach for one of her hands and barreled on.

"The last time we saw each other, I'm afraid I didn't say the right things. I didn't... I thought myself strong, not giving in to the emotions I was feeling for you. Not even allowing us a chance to actually *be* something. But I've realized that's not a strength at all. It's the essence of cowardice, just like you said. And I won't be silenced by fear anymore."

Her eyes shone and she leaned in closer, until I could smell the faint scent of sunscreen and lavender and Ada. Hope was a painfully acute feeling in my chest. "Please, *please*, would you consider forgiving me?"

"I already had," she whispered. "You're forgiven."

Relief flooded through me. "That's good," I murmured. "Thank you."

"But?" she asked, the familiar rise of her eyebrow a shot to my heart.

"How do you feel about me?" I turned my gaze to her hands, small and smooth in mine. There was a faint layer of paint under one of her nails. "I pushed you away in New York because I was afraid. Never because I didn't care about you. Because I do, Ada. So, so much. And I fear that my actions might have made you resent me."

I heard the catch in her breath.

"Grant," she whispered. "I cared about you long before the storage room."

My eyes snapped to her in surprise. Surely she couldn't mean that? But the smile on her face made my heart do a double-take.

"I just didn't realize it for the longest time. Like you, I was afraid to believe what we had could be real. Because real things can be taken away." She reached up and her hands found the back of my neck, blue eyes steadily gazing into mine. I had to swallow, my throat was so dry. "But I'm also done with fear."

The smile on her face echoed mine. "How about we're brave together?"

Ada leaned in so close that I felt her lips move against mine when she replied. "Let's."

Her kiss was home, a warmth and softness I had missed since the last night we'd shared. How had I ever been able to kiss her and not realize immediately what a gift this was? I would never be able to survive without it. What a fool I had been to ever think otherwise.

"You're a treasure," I murmured and she laughed. She was pressed so closely that I felt the beat of her heart, but I wanted her closer still, winding her to me so that all of our surfaces touched.

"I'll take it," she smiled, "if you promise me you'll stay here with me for a few days before you have to fly back to New York."

"Oh baby, I've already texted Adam. He's in charge for the coming week."

Her excited squeal against me was the sweetest sound in the world.

"Ada, do you live here? In this place?"

She shook her head, curls dancing across my neck. "No. I have a small place just a short walk from here. Come with me?"

"There's nowhere else I'd rather be."

28

ADA

It's a bit messy," I said, opening the door to the small two-bedroom apartment I rented. It had been Dr. Willis's suggestion, that I have a place of my own so that Minna and my dad could visit me if I liked.

Grant followed me into the apartment. It was nice, I thought, with large, bright windows with wooden shutters. A woven basket filled with dried lavender sat by the door, a couple of candles on a wooden table. Some of my newer paintings were lined against the walls, an explosion of color.

"There's a lot about me I never told you."

I looked up at him in surprise. "I know. It's okay."

"No. I want you to know."

"All right."

"I was an orphan," he said, quickly. "And I moved around between foster homes often. One to the next."

"Okay," I said softly, moving closer so that I could cover his hand with mine.

"Most were good homes, they just didn't have the time of day for each kid. I got out at eighteen and started working right away. I traded on the stock exchange. I got good at it. But it didn't give me... *anything*."

He was not talking to me but to the wall, as if it was easier to face. As if all of this had been bottled up for so long that it was a struggle to get it out.

"Hey," I said softly. "We can talk about all of this today, now. Or we can wait a bit. I'm not going anywhere."

His hand relaxed under mine and hesitant gray eyes met mine. "I think I have to. Or I never will."

"I'll listen."

"I've always read, since I was a child. Whatever I could get my hands on. I became good at tracking the market and at handling the extreme risk—at making money for money's sake. But that wasn't the life I wanted to live. So I hunted around at museums, at libraries. Tried to find my calling. One day, I bumped into Arthur Hathaway."

I nodded and stroked the back of his hand. "Where?"

"At the Met."

"In the Japanese Reading Room," I breathed.

Grant gave a small smile. "He was meeting with the division head to suggest they list with Hathaway's for a pair of antique sculptures. I only heard half the conversation, listening behind a pillar. But I knew that was what I was going to do. But being close to that kind of art and history, where it all happened? That was the dream. The following four months I spent every waking hour reading up on Hathaway's. All the divisions. I tracked sales and auctions going back months. And then I approached him."

"And he took you up on it."

"I'll never stop being surprised that he did," Grant said, shaking his head. "I had no university education. Nothing."

"You had your intellect. You were a hard worker."

"Maybe, yeah. Yes, I was. But don't you see? I was powerless for so many years. And I made sure I would never, never feel like that again. But I am entirely powerless with you, Ada. And it scared me as nothing had for a very long time."

A hiccupped sob escaped me. "You think I don't feel the same way? I hadn't talked with anyone the way I do with you, not for years. Somehow you reached straight inside and saw everything I tried to hide."

"I don't want you to hide." He reached up and smoothed a tear away from my cheek. "Not from me."

I gave a laugh. "I never could."

"The same for me. You saw through whatever facade I put up."

We smiled at each other, awkward and warm and real. He glanced over at my paintings lining the wall, seeking an easier subject matter. "I didn't know you painted."

"Oh? Well, I used to. I've recently begun again."

"They're good."

"It's fun," I said with a shrug. "I don't expect an 'elusive genius' to think they're any good."

"You read that?" He raised an eyebrow, a grin on his face.

"Yeah. My friend sent me photos of them."

"Hmm. Your friend."

"Yes."

"Does this happen to be the same friend who sent me a copy of *How to Act with Love?*"

I nearly dropped the pot of tea I was preparing. "What?!"

He grinned and took a seat on one of the small wooden chairs at my dining-room table. His legs stretched out long in front of him, too big for the space. "One self-help book on psychology was delivered, neatly packaged, to my concierge. *For Grant Wood,* a note attached said. *I hope this will help you. Life's too short for fear.* Signed by *a friend of a friend.*"

"No way." Minna wouldn't. *She wouldn't.*

"Yep. I read it, too."

"You did?"

"Yeah. Twice, actually."

I sat down opposite him, taking in his dancing eyes. There was no way this was happening. He had flown here. He had apologized. And he had read a psychology book given to him by Minna? Perhaps I should try jumping up and down, to see if the law of gravity still worked.

"It was good."

"I can't believe it."

"So you didn't send it, then? I'll admit I wondered if you had."

"No! Absolutely not. But I know who did." I put my head in my hands.

"Don't be upset with your friend." Grant leaned forward, grabbed my hand again. He ran a finger down the center of my palm. "It helped tell me what I already knew."

"What was that?" I whispered.

"That I'm in love with you. And that I was being an ass about it."

I couldn't help it—tears welled up in my eyes. Suddenly I was in his arms, held against a warm, familiar chest, the scent of him spreading warmth through me.

"I'm so sorry."

"I thought... I thought you didn't, that you didn't see a future with me."

"That's because I was blind. I always *wanted* a future with you, I just didn't think I could have everything I wanted. That it could actually be true."

I pulled back, gazed into the light brown of his eyes. "It can. *It is.* I'm in love with you too, Grant."

He leaned forward until our foreheads met. I could feel the beat of his heart, the strength of emotion. "Oh, Ada."

I reached forward and took his lips with my own. They were soft and gentle against mine, kissing me with yearning. As if he wasn't sure this was really happening.

So I moved over and sat in his lap, my fingers moving up and into his hair. "I'm glad you came here," I murmured against his lips. "So glad."

"I feared you'd send me away."

"Never."

He smiled against me and lifted me up, moving toward the back of the room. We fell onto my small twin bed with laughter, his hands warm as they flitted over my face.

"Ada Hathaway," he declared. "I'm never letting you go again."

I ran a hand down the buttons on his front. "Mmm... What makes you think that's even an option?"

He grinned and bent to press kisses to my neck, my chest, the sweetheart neckline of my linen dress.

"I only have one pressing issue now," he said, looking serious.

"Oh?"

"Your freckles. Are they everywhere? Because I'll find them."

———

"Grant?" I murmured, running my finger up the curve of his bicep. He was lean and taut, muscular in a way that made me feel safe and warm. He was as good outside of his tailored suits as he was inside them.

"Mmm?" He turned against me, tucked me closer to his side. There was an intimate familiarity in the movement, like we'd shared a bed for years instead of a couple of nights, weeks ago. It had been like riding a bike, fitting back in place with him, our bodies remembering each other perfectly.

"I want to stay here for a few more weeks."

"Of course, Ada. You should finish what you came here to do."

"Even if it means we'll be apart for a little while?"

"Even if it means that. I want you to be happy. To get whatever closure you need." He touched warm lips against my shoulder. "Although I'll probably request the same privileges your dad now receives."

"What?"

"Daily calls? Yes, he's told me about that. There's no way I'm not asking for the same."

I laughed in the darkness. "I'll do you one better. I'll call you *twice* daily."

"Perfect."

"It's good, actually. Between us now."

"Oh?"

"I've resented him for so long, for not being there. For not doing more. But he's had his own demons. And he's the only family I have. We need each other."

"You do." He pulled me into his warmth, a leg twining its way between mine. "But he's not the only family you have, Ada."

We settled into the small space, snuggled close together. It might be a tight fit, but I already knew I'd sleep better than I had in weeks.

"Grant?"

"Yes?" Amusement colored his voice.

"Do you know what I've realized?"

"That you love me."

I flushed in the darkness. "Well. Yes. But aside from that."

He ran a hand over my naked waist, fitting me closer to him. "What?"

"Do you remember our fortune cookies?"

"How could I forget?" he said dryly.

"I think we both followed their advice. The fortunes came true."

He laughed softly in the darkness. "You're here for well-organized time and a more well-organized mind?"

"Yes. Although Dr. Willis would probably disagree with the phrasing, so we won't tell the fortune cookie company about that."

"It'll be our secret."

I kissed him, soft and sweet. "And for you, Grant…"

"Love," he said simply. "I learned about love."

EPILOGUE

Two Years Later

"Hi Max," I said, feeling slightly stupid. "It's been a long time now since you left us. I still think about you every day, but it's much better now."

I bent and put a bouquet of flowers on his grave. I had spent a long time at the florist picking them out, until I could almost hear my brother laughing at me. *I don't have all day, Addie. Quit dawdling.* So I'd grabbed a bunch of the brightest, yellowest tulips.

"Guess what? I've married Grant. I can imagine you laughing and laughing at that if you could hear me. But it's true. And I would tell you to stop, because we were wrong about him. He's everything, Max. So good to me—I can't think of a better man. I know you'd think so too if you were still here."

I looked over at the car, where Grant was talking to one of the cemetery gardeners. Always planning and organizing, wherever he went. I smiled and turned back to Max.

"And guess what?" I put a hand over my widening midsection. "We're going to become parents. I guess you could never see that one coming, right? Yourself as an uncle, and me as a mom. But things change. I know you would have been the best uncle, but life wanted something different for us. Don't worry, I'll bore our kids with memories of you, so they'll know about their uncle. I promise to tell them all of your best stories."

Grant walked up the gravel path behind me.

"See? The tulips look great," he said and wrapped his arms around me, one of his hands finding the swell of my stomach. He kissed my neck, just below my ear, and I shivered. His touch never got old.

"How is he?"

I put my hand on top of his, resting together on our son, kicking inside.

"He's good," I said. "He's good now."

WANT MORE OFFICE ROMANCE?

Do you want more forbidden office romances? There are more deliciously powerful men waiting for you in my New York Billionaires series.

Begin the journey with Think Outside the Boss, where Frederica meets a handsome, charming man at a club. They share one hot night together. It's anonymous. It's perfect.

Until she starts her new internship, and discovers her new boss is Tristan Conway... also known as her older, powerful stranger.

Oh, and he wants to see her in his office.

Grab Think Outside the Boss now or read on for the first chapter!

CHAPTER 1
FREDDIE

I'm sorting through junk mail when my fingers gloss over a thick golden envelope. My address is handwritten on the front in sprawling black letters, but there's no name. Mentally, I run through all my friends who might be getting married... no, no and no.

Golden envelope in hand, I sink onto my kitchen chair and flip it over. It has a black wax seal. Stamped into it is a mask, the kind people wear to fancy masquerades in movies. I've never received anything like this.

If this is junk mail, it's gotten very classy.

Can it be to the previous tenant? I've only lived in this studio for a month. Best to make sure... I tear the envelope open with a kitchen knife and pull out a card-stock invitation with gold, printed lettering.

Dear Rebecca Hartford,

It's a new month, and that means new sins to explore. Join us at the Halycon Hotel at ten p.m. the following Saturday and wear the accompanying mask as proof of invitation.

Don't forget that secrecy is fun, phones are not (no one likes a tattle-

tale), and everyone looks better in lace. Or disrobed. But we're getting ahead of ourselves…

Yours in pleasure,
The Gilded Room

Oh God.

I read the invitation twice to sort through all the innuendos.

The Gilded Room? Everyone looks better disrobed? Rebecca Hartford, you minx!

This might be the most elaborate practical joke I've ever been on the receiving end of. Peering into the envelope, I find a mask lined in delicate black silk, two feathers curling above the cut-out eyes like eyebrows. Black jewels crust the bottom half, and three words are written in gold cursive along the edge. *United in pleasure.*

Okay.

Maybe not a practical joke.

I open my laptop and type the Gilded Room in the search bar. A bunch of newspaper articles have been written about the organization, but not a single one of them features pictures. I click open the one entitled *A night in the elite's world of pleasure.*

What I read makes my eyes widen. The Gilded Room is one of New York's best kept secrets, primarily because those in it don't want to be known. They don't want to be seen, heard, and especially not pictured. The Gilded Room guarantees anonymity to its high-flying members, many of whom pay over twenty thousand dollars for their yearly memberships.

I scroll down, my eyes scanning paragraph after incredible paragraph.

Rules are simple. No one is invited that isn't rich, beautiful, or both. Anyone caught with a phone is immediately expelled… and women have all the power at these parties.

There are whispers of politicians attending Gilded Room parties, football players, billionaires and media tycoons... but if they have, the journalist couldn't find anyone willing to talk. It seems this is the only venue among New York's upper echelons where name-dropping *isn't* the norm.

I close my laptop and stare down at the mask and invitation, now lying on my sofa table. Who had Rebecca Hartford been, to be invited to a party like this? I know for a fact that the previous tenant had left the country, my landlord telling me she'd been offered a job in Hong Kong. Contacting her about this feels out of the question.

What if I go myself?

The idea makes me smile. Secret sex parties for the rich? I'm not rich, nor a partier. I am sex-interested, though. It's been a long time since I last...

What am I thinking? Of course I'm not going.

I toss the invitation and the mask in the paper-basket and the lid closes decisively behind them. Besides, I have things to do, like preparing for the internship of a lifetime. I'd worked too hard to get accepted into Exciteur Global's Junior Professionals program, and my first day as a trainee is on Monday.

I have things to do before then.

Get three new pairs of stockings to go with my professional outfits. Unpack the last of the moving boxes. Schedule a time at the DMV to update my driver's license to New York instead of Pennsylvania.

Attend secret sex party is nowhere on that list.

I make it almost an hour and another moving box unpacked before I fish the invitation and mask back out of the paper-basket. Standing in front of the bathroom mirror, I put on the black, feather-adorned mask.

I look moderately pretty. Thick, dark hair, and more than my fair share of it, thanks to my Italian mother. Quite short, but I like to think I'm just petite. Eyes that are a muddy sort of green. It did say you had to be rich or beautiful to get in...

I tug at my ratty old T-shirt to make a V-shaped neckline.

Courtesy of an unusually large chest, I never wear anything that revealing. But I had just unpacked the black dress I got on sale last year. The one that showed a lot of cleavage... Could I pass for Rebecca Hartford? Or at least beautiful enough to gain admission?

"An adventure before the real one starts on Monday," I tell my masked reflection.

———

I once heard it said that women have three forms of showers. The first, a quick body wash. The second, a quick hair and body wash. The third? That's the date-shower, where things get scrubbed and shaven and deep-conditioned.

As it turns out, I've discovered a fourth shower, the help-I'm-going-to-an-elite-sex-party shower. It has a lot of elements from shower number three, like shaving and scrubbing, but includes a few minutes of panicking on the shower floor.

My mind clings to the words I'd read online, that women have all the power. If I don't like it, I'll leave. The Halycon Hotel is one of the nicest in the city, so it's not like I'm walking into an organized crime syndicate.

At least I tell myself that.

It's nearly ten-thirty when I arrive at the hotel. My high heels click on the floor as I walk to the reception. My invitation and mask are both safe and secure in my clutch, ready to be whipped out in lieu of an ID.

"Good evening, miss," a hotel attendant says. His eyes dip to the deep V of my black dress before returning to my eyes.

And *that's* why I usually wear high necklines.

A flush rises on his neck. "You're here for the private party?"

I tug my coat shut. "Yes."

"The elevator to your left," he says, "and straight up to the thirty-second floor. Have fun, miss."

"Thank you." And because I can't resist, I add, "I plan to."

I ride alone in the elevator, my eyes tracking the ever-increasing number of floors on the display. It's become a sure-fire way to keep my fear of heights at bay. Focus on the floors I'm passing and soon enough, it's over. I still breathe a sigh of relief as I step out.

Showtime, Freddie.

I put the mask on and tie the silken strings together, ignoring the way my heart runs amok in my chest with nerves. The scene that awaits me is exceedingly normal. An empty corridor and an open doorway with a pretty, dark-clad woman in front, her face radiating calm professionalism.

She tucks an iPad under her arm. "Welcome, miss."

"Thank you."

"One performance has already concluded, but the next one should be starting just now."

I nod, like I understand what she's referring to. "Terrific, thank you."

She holds her hand out with an expectant look in her eyes. "Right," I say, digging through my clutch to hand her my invitation card. *Don't ask for ID, don't ask for ID...*

But she just looks it over and gives me another smile, this one more friend-to-friend. "Welcome, Miss Hartford. Don't forget to check your phone in on the right, after you enter."

"Of course."

She pushes aside the curtain blocking the door. The contrast is sharp from the bright corridor outside to the dimly lit, smoke-filled rooms beyond. A scent hangs in the air... something thick, like magnolia and incense.

A man dressed only in a pair of black slacks and a tie, no shirt to cover up the broad chest on display, welcomes me. "I'll check your coat, miss."

"Yes, thank you," I say, shrugging out of it. He hangs it up and returns, a hand extended. "Oh! Right." I hand him my phone.

His answering smile makes me think I'm not masking my

nerves as well as I thought. "I'll put your phone right here," he says, opening one of a hundred identical security boxes. "The code is automatically generated, and you'll get a printed receipt with it... here you go. Only you know this. Don't lose it."

"All right," I murmur. "Awesome."

He gives me another encouraging smile, this time tinged with humor. "Enjoy yourself, and remember that we're here at any time if you need help or you have any questions."

"Thank you."

Gripping my clutch tight, I walk into the main space. The first impressions strike me in flashes. White lace and high heels. Drapes of black silk from the ceiling. Men in impeccably fitted suits and dark masks.

People mingle, some standing, some reclining on sofas. A beautiful woman strolls past me in lingerie. It's the imposing kind, with garters and thigh-highs.

"Champagne, miss?" a waiter asks, holding out a tray of flutes. Just like the man working the coat check, he's shirtless.

"Yes, thank you," I murmur. Walking through the throngs of people in a dazed sort of wonder, I think I see people I recognize. It's difficult to tell with the masks, but not impossible, and a few have discarded theirs entirely. One woman is a news anchor and I've seen her on TV dozens of times. A tall, broad-shouldered man has the face of a football player. If I'd been more sports interested, his name would have come to me, but as it is I settle on furtive glances his way. Bottles of champagne with golden labels line an entire wall.

This is wealth like I've never seen it before. It's a rich person's playground, a study in how the wealthy amuse themselves.

Then I see it.

The performance.

There's a raised stage in the middle of the room, and what's taking place on it makes my high school drama club's rendition of *Macbeth* look like child's play. Two lingerie-clad women circle a man on a chair, his hands in cuffs behind him. One runs proprietary nails over the man's sculpted chest, the other sliding her hand up his bare thigh.

My eyes are glued to the scene.

And yet all around me, guests of the Gilded Room continue to mingle in varying states of undress as if three people aren't currently engaged in *very* public foreplay in front of us.

A masked woman in her mid-forties walks past me, pulling a man along behind her by his tie. She shoots me a triumphant look. "The next performance should have pyrotechnics," she says.

I give her a weak smile. "Just what this party needs. Fire."

"I like you!" she calls over her shoulder. "Feel free to join us later!"

Join them, wow. I smile into my champagne and look across the room, hoping to spot more famous people. There is no way my friends will believe me, but I still want to make sure this night turns into the best anecdote possible.

My gaze lingers on a man on the other side of the room. Like most men here, he's in a suit, but he's one of the few not wearing a mask. Not speaking to anyone, either. He just leans against the wall and watches the performance with arms crossed over his chest.

Looks like he's sitting this one out.

I turn in my empty glass of champagne for a full one and lean against the wall opposite him. There's nothing familiar about him, and yet I can't seem to look away.

His gaze snaps to mine, and the laser-focus makes it clear he's well aware of my staring. He raises an eyebrow.

My lips curve into the universal sign of *hi, there.* It's the smile you give a man in a bar to let him know you want him to come over. It's brazen.

A group of guests stop in the middle of the room and it sunders our eye contact. I look down into my champagne with a heart that's suddenly pounding. I'd come here to observe, without any plans of participating...

But a girl can flirt, can't she?

When I see him again, he's no longer alone. A woman runs her hand down his arm in a manner that would be easy to read even if we *weren't* at an elite sex party.

I push off the wall and take a lap of the room. There's a steady, pounding beat emanating from the speakers, heady in its power. More than a few of the mingling guests have moved on from simple conversation, and I pass by a man taking off his partner's bra while discussing New York real estate.

I find a dark corner of the space to retreat to, far away from the couples in varying states of undress. I've never watched other people... well. Perhaps it's time for me to declare this little adventure finished.

That's when he appears by my side, a crystal tumbler in hand.

Brown hair rises over a strong forehead and the square of his jaw covered in two days' worth of stubble. Up close, it's even harder to look away from him.

He raises that eyebrow at me again, but says nothing. He just leans against the wall beside me and we gaze at the crowd in silence.

I take another sip of my champagne to keep my nerves at bay. Who is he? A media mogul? A celebrity I don't recognize? The scion of a political family? For the night, he's a stranger, just like me.

"So?" I ask, watching him through the slitted eyes of my mask. "Are you planning on introducing yourself?"

Read on in Think Outside the Boss!

OTHER BOOKS BY OLIVIA
LISTED IN READING ORDER

New York Billionaires Series

Think Outside the Boss
Tristan and Freddie

Saved by the Boss
Anthony and Summer

Say Yes to the Boss
Victor and Cecilia

A Ticking Time Boss
Carter and Audrey

Suite on the Boss
Isaac and Sophia

12 Days of Bossmas
Christmas Anthology

———

Seattle Billionaires Series

Billion Dollar Enemy
Cole and Skye

Billion Dollar Beast
Nick and Blair

Billion Dollar Catch
Ethan and Bella

Billion Dollar Fiancé
Liam and Maddie

Brothers of Paradise Series

Dark Eyed Devil
Lily and Hayden

Ice Cold Boss
Faye and Henry

Red Hot Rebel
Ivy and Rhys

Small Town Hero
Jamie and Parker

Standalones

Arrogant Boss
Julian and Emily

Look But Don't Touch
Grant and Ada

The Billionaire Scrooge Next Door
Adam and Holly

ABOUT OLIVIA

Olivia loves billionaire heroes despite never having met one in person. Taking matters into her own hands, she creates them on the page instead. Stern, charming, cold or brooding, so far she's never met a (fictional) billionaire she didn't like.

Her favorite things include wide-shouldered heroes, late-night conversations, too-expensive wine and romances that lift you up.

Smart and sexy romance—those are her lead themes!

Join her newsletter for updates and bonus content.
www.oliviahayle.com.
Connect with Olivia

facebook.com/authoroliviahayle

instagram.com/oliviahayle

goodreads.com/oliviahayle

amazon.com/author/oliviahayle

bookbub.com/profile/olivia-hayle

9 789198 793703